MW01601445

*by! Hope you
enjoy the book!
Kate Rizor
Sept 06*

THE
GOVERNOR'S
WIFE

The Governor's Daughter
Copyright © 2005 by Kate Rizor

All rights reserved. No part of this publication may be reproduced or transmitted in any form or by any means, electronic or mechanical, including photocopy, recording, or any information storage and retrieval system, without permission in writing from the publisher.

The Governor's Daughter is a work of fiction. Any resemblance to actual persons and/or events is strictly coincidental. References to actual places and/or historic events are meant to enhance the story and provide a realistic setting for the novel.

Requests for permission to make copies of any part of the work should be mailed to:

Stargazer Press
102-171 Collier Street
Barrie, Ontario L4M 1H6
Canada

Cover and interior design by: Peggy LeTrent
Editing by: Victoria Rosendahl

Library and Archives Canada Cataloguing in Publication

Rizor, Kate, 1976-
    The governor's wife / Kate Rizor.
ISBN 0-9734940-8-5
    I. Title.
PS3618.I94G69 2006   813'.6   C2006-900441-2

Printed in Canada

THE GOVERNOR'S WIFE
By Kate Rizor

~ Book Review ~

Andie or Andra?
Street person or governor's wife?

According to the fingerprints taken after Andie tries to shoplift a bottle of cough medicine, she is the governor's missing wife. The luxurious life Tanner offers beats trying to survive any longer on the streets, she reasons, so why not play along for now?

Tanner doesn't believe for a moment that his defiant, beautiful Andra's been living as a homeless person for 10 years. Even though he suspects her coming forward is an attempt to discredit him, he is going to play along, at least until after the election.

But street life has changed Andie's once-selfish heart. Before she can convince Tanner, the past catches up with them, endangering both her and this man she has come to love.

A suspenseful tale that keeps you rooting for this feisty heroine and her man as they discover what matters most in life—and love.

Bonnie Hearn Hill
Author of *Intern, Killer Body,* and *Double Exposure* for Mira

~ Prologue ~

New York City, New York
December
Ten Years Ago

"I want a divorce."
Tanner Thornburg tested the words aloud for the first time. He had carried them inside two years too long. Tonight he would end it here in their favorite restaurant, Donnelly's.
It was where he had proposed marriage.
It was where he would end it.
But could he do it? He lifted a hand, loosening the tie that had suddenly become too tight. Would he really go through with it this time? He had tried three times before but could never quite get the words out. How do you tell someone you don't love them anymore?
At the sound of shattering glass, Tanner snapped his head up and looked across the restaurant for the source of the sound. His wife stood outside the restroom, hands on hips, the door still swinging behind her. A waitress was hunched at Andra's feet, picking up what looked like broken wine glasses and setting the pieces back on a tray. Glass shards were scattered around Andra's feet, shimmering red, green, blue and yellow from the lights entwined through the decorated Christmas tree outside the restrooms.
Holiday lights blinked from strings of garland criss-crossed on the restaurant's ceiling. The scent of pine from the Christmas tree and the smell of baking bread permeated the room. Flames hissed and popped from the fireplace at the back of the room and music filtered through the restaurant's overhead speakers. Handel's *Hallelujah Chorus*.
It was a time for joy and forgiveness but as the red stain spread across the white cashmere sweater his wife had bought just for this evening, she didn't look particularly forgiving. Her face rivaled the color of the stain. A manager approached and

handed her a washcloth as a peace offering.

Andra's eyes narrowed as she said something to make the waitress burst into tears, push past the manager and race inside the bathroom. Tanner stood to walk over and make amends but Andra turned, stepped over the pool of wine soaking into the white carpet, and walked toward him, her head bent as she furiously scrubbed at the stain.

Tanner sank into his chair. "Is everything all right?"

"Does everything look all right?" Dipping the corner of the washcloth in her glass of water, she leaned her hip against the table and concentrated on her stain. "Merlot. This is never coming out!"

"We'll take it to the dry cleaners."

"And management here is going to pay the bill. I made sure of that!"

"I'm sure you did." Tanner grabbed his glass of water and brought it to his lips. "Why don't you sit down and we can order."

"What do you mean 'order'? We can't stay now. I'm covered with wine!"

"Sit, Andra." It was suddenly quiet, as if the restaurant's volume had just been muted. Utensils stopped clicking against dinner plates. Hushed conversations ceased. Even the classical music playing in the background didn't seem as loud.

Tanner calmly folded his napkin and placed it on his plate as faces turned toward him. "We'll handle it later."

Andra yanked the chair out and sat down, crossing her legs to reveal a small raspberry-shaped birthmark on her ankle before scooting closer to the table. The birthmark had once fascinated him in its uniqueness.

Tanner pushed the menu toward her and she picked it up and began reading it. With her head bent, the soft yellow glow from a hurricane lamp in the center of the table played off brown hair shielding her face. She looked younger than twenty-four and sometimes acted like it—tonight being a prime example.

Christmas. He suddenly realized the bad timing. This was supposed to be the happiest time of the year. Maybe he should wait. But then he tried to think ... when was the last time he had been happy, really happy? It had been... He lowered his head and stared at his plate. He couldn't even remember. Which was why he needed to do this now. Tonight.

"The menu hasn't changed since you left five minutes ago." He was almost spoiling for a fight. That way it wouldn't be so hard to say the four words that would end his marriage. And maybe more. His reputation? His political career?

Her green eyes flashed as fiercely cold as the diamonds in her ears. An anniversary present this year, to which she had responded, *This is a matching set. Where's the necklace that goes with it?*

Tanner fisted his fingers underneath the table. Now. Do it now before you lose your courage.

I want a divorce.

Just say it, he thought, as he caught the eye of their waiter.

I. Want. A. Divorce.

Now before—

A waiter appeared at his side. "Mr. Thornburg." His smile disappeared as he looked at Andra. "Mrs. Thornburg."

"Evening, Pierre." Tanner tried to contain the sigh that rose to his lips. He swallowed it, and around the knot in his throat, said, "How are you tonight?"

Pierre glanced at Andra. "I must apologize for Clarissa, madam. This is her first night—"

"It's no problem," Tanner said before Andra could respond. "It happens to everyone. Now I think we're ready to order, aren't we, Andra?"

Andra snapped her menu shut and pushed it at the waiter. "I'm not very hungry."

Tanner forced a smile. "Well, I'm starving. I think I'll have the roast duck."

"Tonight's dinner is on Mr. Donnelly to show how terrible he feels for what happened tonight."

"Thank Mr. Donnelly but tell him it's not necessary," Tanner said.

"If you insist, sir."

"I do."

Andra straightened but Tanner squeezed her knee under the table and she remained silent as the waiter walked away.

"I don't believe you!" Andra said. "They should do *something* to make up for what happened!"

"It was an accident, now drop it." Tanner took a sip of water. Noticed his hands shaking. He set his glass down and smeared the condensation collecting on the side of the glass. Was this the right place to do this? Shouldn't this be done in private? Maybe he should wait. Just until…no. He had waited long enough.

He cleared his throat. "I—I have something I need to say."

"You haven't changed your mind about running for mayor, have you? Dad's pulled every string to help you make it this far. How many twenty-eight-year-olds do you know running for mayor?"

Tanner glanced up at the red and white poinsettias lining the fireplace mantle. Watched snow whip people's coats as they shuffled past the front window. Anywhere but at her. "I want a divorce."

There. He said it. He held his breath. How would she react? What would she say?

Andra leaned forward, placing her elbows on the red linen tablecloth. "What?"

"I…" Tanner glanced down at the tent-like folded Christmas green napkin perched on his plate. He grabbed it and smoothed it open. Anything to keep his hands busy. "I—I want a divorce." He traced the restaurant's white initials embroidered on the red cloth.

Andra reached over and yanked the napkin away. "What is this really about, Tanner? Is this to get back at me for asking Ron Schultz to work with you? I just thought that he might be a good advisor someday if you should be elected mayor. Dad said he was the best—"

"This isn't about going behind my back to hire Ron."

His face must have revealed the gravity of his words because she whispered, "You...you're not serious, are you?"

"You've changed. I feel like I don't know you anymore."

"But—"

"I haven't been happy. Neither have you."

Andra covered his hand with hers, circling his knuckle with her thumb. It was the first time she had touched him in weeks. "I'm sure it's just the stress of the election coming up, darling. You're so young to run for mayor, you know, and I'm sure it's quite a load to carry around. It'll all be over come election next year."

Almost a year away. How would he last that long? Reporters were already following him; he didn't have a moment of privacy.

Had it been a mistake to accept her father's help? Fresh out of Harvard, Tanner had used his law degree for only one year as an attorney for Smith Bradley and McCoy Associates before turning his eye to the political arena.

"It's not stress and it's not the upcoming election, Andra. It's you. It's us."

"There's counseling—"

"We've tried that." He withdrew his hand from hers. "It didn't work."

"But you—you can't divorce me!"

"You can have whatever you want. I'm not going to fight about this."

"I want you! I want our marriage to work."

"You want what our marriage can bring you, but you don't want me."

"You can't divorce me, Tanner!" She pounded her fist on the table, rattling the silverware. "I've made you what you are today. I've groomed you for mayor of New York City. You would be *nothing* without me and my family!" Andra spoke through clenched teeth.

He bowed his head. She was right. Perhaps he had been too willing to go along with her plans. Like pieces on a chessboard, Andra arranged the people around her to suit her needs.

"You won't ever become mayor if you divorce me." She leaned across the table, her face glowing from the lamp. "I'll see to it!"

"I'm sorry, Andra."

"No, you aren't." She glanced down at her red and white checkered placemat. He knew she wouldn't cry in public. She never had before.

"I'll do anything I can to make this easy on you."

She looked up and he was shocked to see tears in her eyes. "I love you. Don't do this."

It had been a long time since he had heard those words.

"You love my money and what I can bring you but you don't love me."

She was just like her mother. She would rather live a life of fame and fortune than love and happiness. Her mother, Deena, had taught her that when she'd married New York's senator, Roderick Livingston, thirty years ago. The same man who had helped Tanner's rise to power.

Andra had wined and dined him in the beginning, using her charm to work her way into his arms. Into his bed. Into his heart.

He had loved her in the beginning but she'd changed after the wedding ring was on. She was no longer the woman he'd once fallen in love with. Why had it taken Tanner so long to realize this?

Andra shoved her chair back, stood, and with head held high, walked away without saying anything.

Brian Phelps, a new hire materialized at Andra's side. He'd been only a few feet away, watching the restaurant carefully. A month ago, she had been involved in an attempted kidnapping while shopping downtown. While walking out to her car, she had been loading bags in the trunk when she was grabbed from behind. The man attempted to push her into another car but sheer stubbornness prevented him from doing so. She had fought and kicked until she gained the attention of two college students. The man had shoved her away, climbed in his car, and peeled out of the parking lot. They never found him or his vehicle.

Brian's fingers curled around her elbow as he steered her out of Donnelly's. Outside, the Thornburg's Mercedes Benz waited, running. He opened the door. Climbing inside, Andra sank into the heated leather seats as Brian circled the car. He scanned the back parking lot, his brown eyes stopping on the restaurant door. She studied his tense expression and stiff shoulders. He seemed edgy tonight. Definitely nervous. Very rare. Security was usually unflappable at all times.

He climbed in beside her and shut the door with a soft *snick*. She looked back at the restaurant door, expecting to see Tanner come through it, pleading for forgiveness.

Divorce. Tanner wanted a divorce. What if he actually went through with it? What would she do? How would she survive?

She felt tears prick to life but she quickly turned her head away. "Let's go, Brian."

Instead of turning right out of the parking lot, he turned left, toward the highway.

She raised her manicured hand and jerked her thumb in the opposite direction. "Brian, you're going the wrong way. The apartment's that way."

When he didn't reply, she looked over and saw an intense scowl on his face as his concentration wavered between the road and rearview mirror. She saw a small scar above his forehead for the first time, enhanced because of his scowl. Maybe he was circling the block a few times to make sure nobody was following them, she thought, but he continued on until the city lights disappeared.

They must be taking preventive measures and going the long way home, she thought. They rode in silence for ten minutes before she finally spoke up.

"Where are we going?"

"Shut up."

She looked over at him. "What did you say?" Nobody had ever talked to her that way. And she would see to it nobody would start. Especially the hired help.

He glanced over and her breath caught when she saw the coldness in his eyes. "I said *shut up.*"

"What are you doing, Brian? Stop the car right now!"

"I demand you stop this car!"

She didn't see his fist in the darkness but felt it as it made contact with her jaw. Her head popped back, jolting against the window. She cried out and massaged her wound.

"What are you doing? Where are you taking me?" she opened the flap of her purse and rummaged through it for her cell phone. Lipstick. Comb. Wallet. Come on, *where was her cell?*

Brian ripped her purse off her lap. The window whined as it was lowered. He chucked her purse out of the car.

"What do you want?" she whispered, edging closer to her door. "Money? I've got money."

"You aren't worth what's on the bottom of my shoe, lady. But I'll take whatever they'll give me for you." She almost didn't recognize his voice.

"It was you, wasn't it? You were the one who tried to grab me at the mall that day."

Brian rubbed his thigh. "You nearly put a hole in my leg with those damn heels you were wearing. And I'll make you pay for it before the night is through."

She leaned away, huddling against the door. "Brian, please stop this. Let me go and I won't say anything to Tanner. I promise."

"Another empty promise, Andie? Like the ones you give to Thornburg?"

"Tanner threatened to divorce me, so if you think you're going to get ransom—"

"Oh, he'll pay. He has to, because what will his beloved city think of him if he doesn't? What will that bastard of a father

you have think of his only son-in-law if he doesn't?"
The Pennsylvania state line came and went. My God,
where was he taking her? What would he do with her? The
paved road suddenly gave way to dirt as they went through road
construction. Large, orange-flashing barrels forced the road
from two lanes to one, causing them to slow. The Mercedes'
tires churned up loose gravel which snap-popped as it hit the
wheel wells.
She grabbed the door handle, ready to spring out. She
would suffer some cuts and bruises, maybe a few broken bones,
but she would be—
Brian reached out and attempted to grab her elbow but
she moved and he swiped at empty air. The sudden movement
caused him to lose control of the steering wheel. She felt the
car sliding to the left. He tried to correct it but saw another
barrel coming up too fast, too close. He swung the steering
wheel in the other direction, trying to avoid the collision—and
did—but sent them into a fishtail on the loose gravel.
He slammed on the brakes. It was like trying to stop on
ice. A cloud of gravel dust enveloped the car from the sudden
brakes and she cried out when she felt the car pitch to the side.
Her head slammed against the window as the car began rolling
through the brush like a mad bull set loose from the chutes.
She saw the world spinning crazily, heard the airbags engage,
felt her head pop back from the sudden blow—the material
scraped her face—before she felt nothing.

~ One ~

Detroit, Michigan
November, Present Day

She stumbled up to the front desk of the emergency room
and sagged against the counter, legs shaking from the effort it
took to cross the room.
"I…I need to see a doctor. Please, it—it's an emergency."

The woman behind the counter glanced up. "What's wrong this time, Andie?"

"I—I can barely breathe, Joyce." Andie lowered her head and coughed deeply into her hand, her body shaking violently from the sound. "And my chest…my chest really hurts."

The woman glanced briefly at a sign posted on the wall: *If You Are Experiencing Chest Pain, Please Notify the Front Desk Immediately.*

She bowed her head, rubbing the pain flaring between her eyes. She was achy all over; even her bones ached. "Look, I know what you're thinking, but I'm for real this time, Joyce," knowing she had said that same thing two weeks ago when she had come in for a slight fever.

Joyce pushed a clipboard and form over the counter. "Name, address, social security number."

"Come on, Joyce. You know I don't have some of those."

Joyce turned away and started flipping through paperwork stacked in her in-box. "Bring it up front when you're done."

She slapped her hand against the bullet-proof glass that shielded Joyce. "Please, Joyce, something is seriously wrong!"

The sudden outburst made Joyce jump in her seat and glare up at her. "Andie, there are a lot of people who have been waiting longer and are in more serious need of medical attention than you."

She looked over her shoulder at the people sitting in the waiting room. At this time of night, on a cold one like this, the room was packed with vagrants like herself. She saw Jon, who had been kicked out of his apartment when he couldn't afford the thirty dollar increase his landlord had demanded. Not with his diabetes and not on his SSI check. He had been homeless ever since.

She saw a homeless family she knew, the Brown's or the Braun's, something like that. Their kid was sick, leaning against his dad. His cheeks were ruddy and red, his eyes watery. Probably an allergy. The kid kept her awake in the shelters some nights with his chronic sneezing and sniffling.

She coughed again and winced as sharp pain bit her ribs. "How—how long do you think it'll be?"

"Some of these people have been waiting over two hours."

"Two hours! I can't wait two hours." She leaned against the counter, using it to support her weight. She looked across the room and tried to judge the distance to the nearest chair. She didn't know if she could make it.

"I'm sorry, but you'll have to either wait your turn or you can go down to the nearest Walgreen's and get something for that cold of yours."

"It's not a cold this time."

The Weather Channel murmured from a TV mounted in the corner of the waiting room. A meteorologist predicted another chilly November night.

She lowered her head and coughed again. Oh God, not another one. She had barely survived the cold last night, after spending two hours trying to find a place to sleep. Helping Hands Ministry down the road had been full. The overcrowded First Presbyterian Church had closed its doors early.

Forced to walk along the Detroit River, she looked for a doorway nook, a park bench, a freeway overpass, anywhere to rest her head and try to recover. She had finally bunked down in the corner of an alley.

She was tired, sick and not in the mood to be given the run-around tonight.

Andie pressed her elbows on the counter. "Is this because I don't have insurance?"

"Andie, if you please sit down the doctor—"

She swept her hand toward the waiting room. "You make these people wait for hours and then when they're lucky enough to get in back, the doctor barely looks at them before sending them on their way! This is no way to treat people!"

"I'll call Security if you don't calm down!"

"This is discrimination!"

Joyce picked up the phone and punched the one key she was familiar with: Security.

"Bob, this is Joyce in Emergency. We need someone down here immediately."

She whirled around and used the wall for support as she made her way toward the doors. She heard shouts behind her but didn't stop until she was outside.

The donated jacket she wore was not enough to contain the chills wracking her body. She clutched it closer and lurched away from the brick wall, stumbling toward the street.

The bitter night pierced her lungs, making it painful to breathe. Once around the corner of the building she hesitated, leaning against the wall to catch her breath before making her way around the hospital and down the street.

People passing her on the cracked sidewalk edged closer to the street as she stumbled by. She must look like a crazy woman—or a drunk—with her breath coming in short gasps, her shoulders hunched from the constant throbbing between her shoulder blades.

Walgreen's was ahead, about two blocks.

She hoped she could make it that far.

~~~~

"Ma'am, may I help you find something?"

She looked up as a store employee approached her, a price gun clutched against his leg. She could tell by his baby-smooth face that he was young, probably still in high school.

Youth. Innocence. A life not even fully experienced yet. What she wouldn't give to have that. Have the security of knowing that you had somebody to take care of you, a warm meal every night, a roof over your head. A warm bed.

"No, thanks. Just looking," she narrowed her eyes at his name tag. "Josh."

"Okay, let me know if I can help."

But he didn't leave. She stiffened as his eyes trailed slowly down her jacket. Was he looking at her in attraction or revulsion? She had run into both in the ten years she had been living on the streets.

Then his lips twitched in a half-smile, half-grimace. She had her answer.

"Thanks though." A verbal hint to leave. And when that didn't work, she began coughing again, which did the trick.

"No problem." He hurried away, returning to a box that sat at the other end of the aisle. He stopped, stooped over and reached inside, grabbed a box of Band-Aids and started pricing them. She caught him looking at her again before he returned his attention to the box.

She didn't care what he or anyone else thought of her. She hadn't had a chance to wash before being kicked out of the shelter three nights ago after pulling a knife on a man who had slipped into the woman's bathroom to sneak a peek—and maybe something more—while she was using the restroom. *"We don't want any trouble here, Andie."* She was escorted out the door. Emily's Place maintained a "three-strikes-you're-out" rule. She stayed there when it wasn't over capacity. The two earlier warnings included stealing and drug possession. The stealing was true, the drugs were a set-up. Three weeks ago, the employees were notified that someone staying there was involved with drugs so they searched everyone's belongings. Stan needed somewhere to stash his drugs. She saw him put them in her backpack, setting her up for the fall. She fled before the cops could get there.

She trailed her hand over the products on the shelf. Robitussin, Sudafed, Benadryl. She returned each one to the shelf when she saw the prices. Too expensive. She couldn't afford them.

Her legs shook again so she dropped to one knee to rest and continued looking at the dozens of over-the-counter drugs. There were some for sinuses and some for colds, some for allergies and others for the flu. Which one did she want?

She reached for a bottle of generic cold medicine and looked at the price. It was still too expensive. Sticking her hand in her pocket, she gathered the loose change she had been tossed while sitting outside Emily's Place last night. Eighty cents. It was all she had left after buying some underwear yesterday.

She sighed, dropped the change back in her pocket, and stood, looking left and right. Nobody around.

Tucking the medicine in a coat pocket, she waited a minute before heading toward the front of the store. She was four, three, two steps from the door. Almost there.

One more step and she'd be free. She breathed a sigh of relief as she passed through the doors.

"Ma'am?"

"Shit."

~ Two ~

Andie winced as the handcuffs tightened around her wrists.

Officer Tyler Mason finished reading her Miranda rights and said, "Do you understand your rights, Andie?"

"Yes, but I—I didn't do anything, Mason!" She closed her eyes as chills crawled over her skin. She had never been arrested before. Tickets and warnings, yes, but not an arrest. Maybe it wouldn't be so bad. It would mean a roof over her head. A night without worrying about being attacked while she slept. A visit from a nurse?

"Get in back." He nudged her toward the open back door of a black and white police cruiser. "And watch your head."

"I forgot I had that stuff in my pocket," she insisted again as she ducked into the back seat. "I was going to pay for it."

"Sure you were."

"I didn't steal it!"

"Like I don't hear that every day. Now watch your feet."

She tucked her feet inside as he shut the door. She watched through the window as Mason turned to the store manager leaning against the brick building, shook his hand and walked around the cruiser.

Collapsing against the worn seat, she pulled her legs up

to her chest to try to stay warm in the rapidly cooling car. It smelled of old urine and vomit.

She closed her eyes and concentrated on taking deep breaths but erupted into another fit of coughing. Andie hung her head, dark hair shielding her face.

Mason opened the door and sank behind the wheel, adjusting the rearview mirror, revealing hooded blue eyes and eyebrows already turning gray. He was only in his late thirties but the wrinkles creasing his forehead and cheeks made him appear much older, as if he scowled too much. She suspected there were very few smiles in a job like his.

"You don't look so good, Petersen. You have a rough night?"

She closed her eyes. "I—I'm sick."

Slipping his hands into leather gloves, he cranked up the heat. "Better?"

"It—it'd be—be better if you take these—these cuffs off." Damn cold. She couldn't stop shaking.

"I can't this time, Andie. I'm sorry." Mason started to shift his car in gear but stopped, glancing back at her again. "Ah, hell," he said before putting the car in park again. He opened his door and walked to the back of the cruiser.

The back door popped open and he leaned in, settling a blanket around her shoulders. It was old and faded but clean-smelling.

"Thanks Mason."

She knew Mason well by now. He worked the night shift and responded to many calls involving her either being victim or victimizer. Unfortunately, it was usually the latter, like the times she'd been caught for pickpocketing, loitering or shoplifting. But there was one time when she was attacked in an alley and almost raped before Mason arrived, scaring away her attacker.

He'd never officially arrested her, letting her off with a warning each time with the excuse that the jails were already too overcrowded. After responding today to the shoplifting call, he took one look at her and simply shook his head, and strangely, she'd felt guilty at disappointing him.

Unlike other officers who had harassed her in the past, Mason was nothing but kind to her, offering her names, addresses and phone numbers of shelters where she could stay. "Just until you get on your feet," he'd told her. "And get out of this city before it kills you."

She looked out the window as the city blocks passed. "I can't believe you arrested me for taking some medicine. Don't you have any compassion?"

"It must be your lucky day because the manager decided not to press charges."

"Then why am I being arrested?"

"There's a warrant out for your arrest."

"What—" she coughed "—for?"

"You never showed up for your hearing on your drug charges at Emily's Place."

"Because the drugs weren't mine! That frickin' idiot—"

"You still have to show. It's not like you're too busy, you know. I thought we had this discussion before."

"What discussion?" The blanket started to slip off her shoulders but she couldn't stop it with her hands cuffed. It pooled at her feet. The chills returned in full force.

"About you getting off the streets. Finding a job. Making a life for yourself."

"Who's going to hire someone like me? It's not like I have references or a work history. No computer to even *do* a resume."

"There's the library."

"Even if I had computer access, I don't have any work history."

Not that I can remember, she wanted to say but didn't.

"You must have somewhere you can go. There must be someone back home, someone who loves you."

Home. He didn't know how much she wished that to be true. But where was home? Her life as she had known it started ten years ago when she awoke in a hospital outside

Milford, Pennsylvania. Her mind and memory were as muddy as the clothing in which she'd been found. Her husband, Brian Petersen, had been standing attentively at her side. But it didn't seem to be concern that made him refuse to leave her alone. He'd seemed nervous every time the doctors or nurses came in, every time they asked questions about her. *What is her name? Date of birth? Address? What is her medical background? Is she allergic to anything?* He seemed more concerned about getting her out of the hospital than with her recovery. Brian turned down the nurses' offers to bring her the daily newspaper and refused her requests to watch the nightly news, claiming that the daily drudge of news would only heighten her agitated state.

Despite doctor's protests, he signed the discharge papers only four days after she'd awakened from a coma caused by the automobile accident. The accident had almost claimed her life. After leaving the hospital, they'd traveled west all day and stopped for the night in Detroit.

She should not have left with him. From the beginning, her instincts screamed that something was wrong with him. Her intuition proved right the fourth night out of the hospital when he tried to force himself on her. She'd managed to escape, still bruised and battered.

Her life before that day was as blank as the street beggars' faces. How old was she? Where was she from? Did she have family who missed her? What had life been like before that fateful day ten years ago?

Answers eluded her.

Detroit had been her only home since. She survived by pickpocketing wallets from unsuspecting men. Shoplifting food, medical supplies and other necessities. Living every day wondering if it would be her last. Never trusting anyone or establishing friendships for fear that she'd be betrayed and turned into the authorities.

Or killed.

Don't trust anybody; it was her rule after the incident with

Brian. *Because if she couldn't trust her own husband, who could she trust?* Always stay alert and don't sleep too deeply. And never carry money for more than a day. Money should be spent immediately. If it wasn't, you were a target.

Police were suspicious of her story; how she wished she were lying.

"We're here." Mason swung the steering wheel and turned into the parking lot of the police station.

She eyed the station for the first time. "What's gonna happen?"

"You'll be processed and brought before a judge to explain your side of the story."

"I was set up. Stan put those drugs in my bag."

"Tell that to the judge."

"Come on, Mason. Don't do this. Please!"

"I've been too lenient on you, girl. Maybe being arrested will wake you up." He climbed out and helped Andie from the back seat. His gloved hand curled around her elbow as he steered her inside. They rode the elevator downstairs. Mason guided her to an orange vinyl-covered chair, cracked from decades of use, oozing white-gray stuffing.

"Here, sit."

She sank into the chair and winced. "Can you loosen the cuffs?"

"Soon. Would you like to make a phone call in a few minutes?"

She glared up at him. "Who would I call?"

Mason shrugged. "Can I trust you to stay here while I talk to Officer Jones?"

She refused to look at him.

"Andie?"

She heard him sigh and looked up once he turned his back. He walked up to a female officer who sat on a stool behind the desk, clenching a steaming coffee mug in one hand, a newspaper in the other.

A large, yellowed city map was tacked to the mint-green

wall behind her. A collage of newspaper clippings were taped on the other wall. Her eyes skimmed the headlines that announced decreases in murders, increases in identity theft, and budget cuts within the police department. The room smelled like old coffee that had sat untouched for too long.

"Evening, Jan. How are you?" Mason pressed his hip against the desk, his hand resting on the butt of his gun.

She lifted her head from the article she was reading. "Okay, Ty, you?"

"Good as can be expected, I guess." Mason jerked a thumb toward her. "Got an Andie Petersen here on a warrant."

"Full name?"

"Unknown."

"Age?"

"Unknown."

"Birthday?"

Mason cleared his throat. "Uh, unknown."

Jones lifted an eyebrow. "What *do* you know about her, Mason?"

He looked over his shoulder and caught her looking at him. "She claims she suffered from amnesia ten years ago after a bad car accident. Doesn't remember anything before then."

"If we had a nickel for every time we heard that." She closed the newspaper. "What's she here for?"

"Has a warrant for drug charges."

Jones stepped over to the computer and pulled the keyboard closer. "Name again?"

"Petersen, Andie. Petersen with an 'e'."

Jones punched a few buttons on the computer. "Looks like she's had a number of tickets and run-ins with the law. But no arrests."

"This is her first."

"You'll need to take off the cuffs so I can fingerprint her."

Jones began filling out paperwork as Mason leaned against the desk and filled her in on the details of her arrest.

He pulled the newspaper closer as the paperwork wrapped up. Open to page three, the bottom of the *Detroit Free Press* had a headline that read, "NY Governor's Wife Still Missing After Ten Years—Police No Closer to Solving Andra Thornburg's Mysterious Disappearance."

Mason started the article but stopped when his eyes drifted to the head and shoulders shot of Governor Tanner Thornburg's wife. He leaned closer. The woman looked familiar. Dark hair. Almond-shaped eyes. A beautiful woman except for her eyes. They were cold, filled with secrecy and suspicion.

It looked like...

It couldn't be. He studied the name.

Andra Thornburg. Andra.

Andie?

Just a coincidence? It had to be.

Mason picked up the paper, studying the picture. The woman had much shorter hair. The picture was grainy.

His eyes drifted to Andie, who sat slumped in the chair. Her eyes were closed; she looked to be asleep. Her head bobbed once before she jerked upright, her eyes opening in alarm as she battled slumber.

He was imagining things but he had to be sure.

"Jan?"

"Yeah?"

Mason pushed the newspaper across the desk. "Can you call the New York PD and ask for Andra Thornburg's case file, photograph and fingerprints? This photo is a bit grainy."

"Sure. What do you want me to do once I have them?"

"I want you to compare Andra's fingerprints with Andie's."

~ Three ~

New York City, New York
Four Days Later

"Governor?"

Tanner Thornburg looked up from the morning's front

page headline in the *New York Times*—"Cold Case Team Revisits Ten-Year Disappearance of Governor's Wife"—to meet the dark eyes of Ed Carlson. A moment passed before he recognized the FBI agent assigned to Andra's disappearance so long ago.

Ed Carlson had lost a lot of weight since he'd last seen him two years ago. His face was slimmer, his beard gone. For once he didn't smell like cigarette smoke. Perhaps he had quit.

He dropped the newspaper on the table and stood, offering his hand. "Agent Carlson, good to see you. What brings you here on a Sunday morning?"

Ed Carlson shook the governor's hand. "I hope I'm not interrupting you, sir. I went next door to see if you were home but was told I'd just missed you. The man at the front desk said I could find you here."

"I'm pretty predictable, I guess," Tanner laughed and leaned over, removing his briefcase from the chair beside him. He had stopped briefly in the Starbucks café beside his apartment building to grab a coffee and cinnamon roll before heading to the Governor's Mansion in Albany.

He glanced out the window as his driver pulled up to the curb. "Please sit." He resisted the urge to look at his watch. From New York City, it would take over two hours to get to Albany.

Carlson saw him look over at the Mercedes. "Is this a bad time? I just received news that I thought you'd want to hear in person."

"I was on my way home, but if you have news about Andra, my schedule is now wide open."

Both the New York State Capitol and the governor's executive mansion, a large Queen Anne located on Eagle Street, were in Albany. After being elected, Tanner had moved into the Governor's Mansion but sometimes returned on weekends and holidays to the penthouse apartment he owned in New York City.

He awoke early that morning to miss heavy traffic.

His fingers hesitated over Andra's picture in the top right corner of the newspaper. Dark eyebrows fanned even darker almond-shaped eyes. Lips that produced a frown more often than not. Skin the color of sand and just as bristly. A body more heady and tempting than the perfume on it. She had been beautiful; her personality had made her ugly.

"Is this about reopening the case?" he folded the newspaper and tucked it in his briefcase, wishing he could do the same with his memories of ten years ago. The restaurant. The threat of divorce. The argument. The uncertainty when he arrived home that night to find her missing.

"We have news about your wife," Carlson said. "For once, nothing was leaked to the press about it."

Your wife. The words sounded foreign. With the anniversary of her disappearance days ago, he had buried himself in work, hoping to forget what had happened so long ago.

One day had passed. Maybe she had taken off for a few days to cool down, perhaps to worry him. He called her parents by the second day to see if she'd stopped by. He went out to look for her when his anger turned to concern.

He had returned alone.

His former bodyguard, Brian Phelps, disappeared the same time as his wife. Phelps was wanted for questioning but was never found. The FBI entered the picture when the Mercedes Benz was found across state lines.

Tanner had remained single since. He'd rushed into marriage before and learned from his first mistake.

He crossed his arms. "What about her?"

"We found her."

Tanner closed his eyes. Andra's body had finally been found. Now he could give her a proper burial and have peace of mind. He might finally have all of his questions answered. What if she had suffered? What if she'd been tortured? What if she had been raped?

What ifs had tortured him all these years. Lying awake at night, wondering what she'd gone through. What if she had suffered? What had he been responsible for?

Tanner met the agent's eyes. He struggled with the next question, not knowing if he wanted the answer or not. "How—how did she die?"

"She's alive."

"It's just another false claim."

"This one is the real deal."

"That's what you said about the others." Carlson had followed up on the thousands of leads over the years, some as far away as Paris. Fingerprints had ruled them all out.

The women who pretended to be Andra looked and acted like her – hair as dark as coffee and just as rich smelling, beautiful clothing that looked drab and cheap compared to the woman, and arrogance stronger than her temper. But when Tanner looked closer at their pictures, there was something missing in their eyes – the shrewdness Andra had so perfected. And they were all missing Andra's birthmark, a small raspberry-shaped birthmark on her ankle.

Even after ten years, he continued to search for her because it was his duty, one of the most important characteristics Tanner's father had drilled into his only child since birth. Tanner's strength of character was behind his rise to fame and power, the foundation of his popularity. New York's citizens trusted and admired his strong morals. What would they think if he quit searching?

"Her fingerprints came back a match. It's her."

Tanner lifted his head. His mouth opened but no words came out. Was it possible they had found Andra this time? It was hard to dispute fingerprints.

"What—what is she doing? Where has she been all these years? Why didn't she ever call or write?"

"Detroit."

"I—I have to see her. Now. I have to see for myself."

If it was her, he'd call his assistant, Elizabeth Van Dyke, and tell her he might not be returning to Albany for some time. He would have to take a break from his job. He'd stay in

New York City until he could get everything settled.

Carlson looked up. "She was—"

A blender buzzed in the background. Tanner waited until it became quiet again before he said, "What? I didn't hear you."

Carlson looked away, not wanting to tell him what his wife had become.

A street beggar.

A thief.

And now a criminal sitting behind bars.

~ Four ~

He hadn't been this nervous since his wedding day.

Tanner pulled on his tie as he paced the interrogation room of the downtown Detroit police station and looked up at his bodyguard, Jared McPherson. Jared had been his best friend since they were six-year-old neighbors, growing up in Syracuse. After Brian Phelps' mysterious disappearance ten years ago, Tanner had hired Jared; he was the only one he trusted.

"Relax," Jared said, taking the chair nearest the door. "You're about as strung as—"

"Wouldn't you be?" Tanner sank into a chair at the table and leaned forward, resting his elbows on his knees and clasping his hands prayer-like in front of him. He bowed his head and stared at the floor.

The small room was unnaturally dark due to a burned out light bulb. It was simply furnished with a scarred, wooden table and four chairs. Ventilators hummed above as the heat kicked on, stirring Tanner's hair. A clock ticked loudly above the door, reminding Tanner how long he'd been waiting.

Since receiving news that Andra was positively identified, he had not been able to sleep or concentrate on work, gripped by the unknown. What would she look like? How would she act? Would she remember him?

During the short flight from New York to Michigan, he

thought of all the questions he wanted to ask her: Why did you leave? What have you been doing all these years? Most of all, will you come back? But did he want to know the answers? Did he *want* her to come back? Would she want to return? Maybe she left for a reason. Maybe she didn't want to be found. Maybe he just made things worse by coming here today.

Too many maybes, too little information.

Ten years ago, he mentioned divorce. Would he go through with it after all this time? Did he still love her? Would they be able to start again, start fresh?

He didn't know what he wanted from their marriage or if it would even be possible to have one again. But he knew he wanted two things: answers, and to see that she was alive and well. Anything else was trivial. Maybe after today he could finally lay his guilt to rest.

They'd been escorted into an interrogation room but nobody had returned to talk to them.

After thirty minutes, Tanner glanced at his Rolex. Maybe something was wrong. Had she changed her mind about seeing him? What if—

Tanner stood as the door opened. A blond man who had to be nearly six-four or six-five—he ducked as he stepped inside the room—was dressed in a wrinkled, blue dress shirt and striped tie that was tied ridiculously short. If his height wasn't intimidating, his handshake surely was as he reached out and grasped the governor's hand.

"Governor, welcome to Michigan," he said. "I'm Captain John Logan." He swept his hand toward a police officer who entered the room and shut the door. "This is Tyler Mason, the officer who identified your wife."

Tanner shook Mason's hand. "You don't know how long I've been waiting for this day."

"Please, sit." Logan took the chair across from the table.

Tanner sank back down and looked between the two men. "Is she here?"

"She's here," Logan replied.

"Can I see her? Is she okay?"

"Before we bring her in, I'm going to have Mason bring you up to speed."

Mason pulled a folder closer, thick with papers of all sizes and colors. "Governor, sir—"

"Call me Tanner, please."

Mason cleared his throat. "Governor, there's something you should know about Andie."

Tanner lifted his eyebrow. "Andie? You mean Andra?"

"She goes by Andie Petersen," he said. "And she doesn't know you're here today. She—"

"Petersen? Andie Petersen? Why—"

"Governor, this will be quite difficult for Officer Mason to say," Logan said. "We promise to answer any questions you might have after—"

"Of course. I'm sorry. Please, go on."

Mason leaned forward and pressed his hands on the table as if trying to summon the right words. When he took his hands away, a sweaty palm print remained. Tanner stared as it evaporated.

"I'm not quite sure how to say it gently, Governor. I mean, we're still trying to put together the pieces and from what we can tell—"

"Tyler, start from the beginning," the captain said. "It might help."

Tanner was suddenly too hot in his suit. He unbuttoned his suit jacket and tried to breathe around the panic in his throat. What weren't they telling him? Several possibilities entered his thoughts at once. Was she re-married? Did she have children, a different life now? Was she injured? Was his wife a vegetable, unable to care for herself? What? *What was so difficult to say?*

Mason finally lifted his head. "I've known Andie now for almost ten years, ever since I was fresh out of the academy. I see her a lot on the streets."

"She works downtown?"

Mason glared at the table, his forehead furrowing. Tanner could see the man was struggling to be tactful so he leaned forward and met the officer's eyes. He couldn't keep quiet any longer; he had to *know*.

"Officer, please, whatever you're trying to say, just say it. You're killing me here."

Mason looked almost relieved. "Governor, sir, there's something you should know about your wife." He proceeded to tell Tanner everything he wanted to know.

And some things he didn't.

~~~~

Andie jerked awake as her cell door popped open. She sat up from the lumpy cot that had seen too much use and rubbed the sleep from her eyes. Despite the women chatting from inside surrounding jail cells, she'd had more rest in the last few days than she'd had in a month.

Tyler Mason stood in the open doorway, a clipboard pressed against his hip.

She swung her feet to the cement floor. "What's wrong?"

"How are you feeling?"

Peeling paint crackled as she leaned against the yellow wall. "Better."

After being booked, a doctor visited, listened to her lungs, ordered X-rays, and diagnosed her with pneumonia. After taking antibiotics throughout the weekend, she could already feel the effects. Her chest and back still ached and she still suffered from shortness of breath at times but the horrible cough was subsiding.

Mason stepped inside the cell. "The drug charges have been dropped."

"What?"

"The fingerprints on the bag weren't yours and a witness came forward, who saw a…"—he consulted his clipboard—

"… Stan Jensen stashing the drugs in your bag."

Andie slipped off the mattress and dragged herself to her feet. Instead of relief she felt disappointment. This would mean no more roof over her head. No more regular meals. No more security, knowing she could close her eyes without worrying about being attacked in her sleep.

"No, no, they *were* mine, Mason."

"A few days ago you said they weren't."

"I was wrong. I'm finally admitting to my mistakes. Isn't that what you always tell me to do?"

"Come with me. We have to talk."

She couldn't go back out there. She wouldn't be able to survive the approaching winter. Shelters were already filling up. Some were closing from lack of state funding. Where would that leave her? Out on the streets again? Underneath an overpass or bridge?

If she stepped out those doors, she would not live to see the spring.

"Come on, Petersen, let's go."

She backed up until her shoulders were pressed against the bars. "If you put me back out there, I'll do something to be put right back in here, Mason, I swear I will!"

"You might not have to go back on the streets." Lifting his hand, he motioned for her to come out. "Come with me and I'll explain."

"I know what you're doing and I'm not going through any more job skills training. I made a fool of myself the last time I suffered through an interview and I'm not—"

Mason sighed and grabbed Andie, spinning her around. "I'm sorry but you made me do this." He pushed her against the bars and grabbed her wrists behind her back, slapping on handcuffs.

"I don't want to go back out there!" Andie dug her heels against the floor as he tried to push her forward.

"Andie, for God sake, if you'd only let me—"

"I don't want to go, please, Mason!" She battled tears

and won. She learned long ago that men took advantage of you—sexually, physically, emotionally—when your defenses were down. Since the accident, she'd broken down only once in front of her husband, Brian. His hand, once a comforting touch, turned to a groping one followed by pain when she pushed him away.

Mason walked her down the hallway, up a flight of stairs and stopped outside a closed door labeled Interview Room #1. Mason turned her around and took off the cuffs.

"There's someone in here I want you to meet."

"Who?"

"Your husband. Why didn't you ever tell me you were married?"

"B—Brian? Brian's here?"

"Brian? What? No, it's—"

More memories of her husband surfaced. Brian in the motel, climbing on top of her, his hand sliding under her shirt as she lay on the bed recovering from the accident. Trying to push him off her, her cries as he backhanded her across the face. Her clothing tearing as he tried to rip her shirt off. Reaching for the phone beside the bed and bringing it down on top of his skull. Fleeing into the night.

"No. I can't go in there. I—I can't see him." She turned to run but Mason clamped a hand around her elbow.

~ Five ~

Andie entwined her fingers on the tabletop as she eyed the closed door. Her husband would enter any minute, Mason had said in a voice that sounded suspiciously like a warning.

After her escape attempt, Mason moved her to a separate interview room to calm down, which was only large enough to hold a table and two chairs. White walls were covered with dirty fingerprints. The vinyl floor was sticky beneath her slippers, which the station had issued upon her arrest. She heard the floor give up its hold on her slipper as she crossed her legs.

Andie glanced at the clock on the wall. She'd been waiting nearly half an hour. What was going on? What was taking so long? How had Brian found her? And what was he going to do now that he had?

She held her breath when the door opened. Voices filled the room. Tyler Mason's was the only one she recognized. She lowered her head and dug at a crack in the table, refusing to look up.

"You have her in handcuffs?" A soft, deep voice, filled with power and authority, reached Andie's ears.

A voice that expected to be obeyed.

A voice that was not Brian's.

Andie frowned. Where had she heard that voice before? She tried to remember, but nothing surfaced.

"We had to restrain her, sir. She almost took off when we mentioned her husband was here." Mason dropped a hand on her shoulder. "Andie, look who's here to see you."

Andie swallowed and shifted her eyes to the source of the voice.

Dark eyes. Darker eyebrows framed by the darkest, longest eyelashes. A slender, well chiseled nose. A mouth made for kissing, she thought. Full and wide, dangerously close to being sensual. The jaw and chin were stubborn, full of male pride.

Not Brian.

Not Brian.

A stranger. He stood in the doorway, dressed in a navy blue pin-striped suit that stretched tautly over broad shoulders. She tried to convince herself that his cologne did not reach her from this far away and that her pulse did not quicken from the intoxicating scent. But the lies were difficult to swallow around the knot in her throat.

Andie narrowed her eyes. "Do I know you?"

Mason glanced at the stranger in surprise. "This is Tanner. Your husband? Surely you remember—"

She pictured Brian's ugly mug—the pockmarked ruddy

cheeks, the caterpillar-like uni-brow—and said, "This isn't my husband. I don't know who he is." She would have remembered this man's face anywhere.

The man pulled the chair out across from her and sank into it. "Can you leave us for a few minutes, Officer Mason? And can you take the cuffs off? I don't think they'll be necessary."

"But, sir, she's—"

"She's not an animal," Tanner said. "She's my wife."

"I'm not your wife!" Andie rose to her feet but Mason, who stood behind her, placed his hands on her shoulders and pushed her back in the chair.

Mason reached for the handcuffs but Andie pulled away. "You're not gonna leave me alone with him, are you?"

"He's your husband." Mason slipped the handcuffs off and tucked them on his belt before heading toward the door. "I'll be right outside if you need me, sir."

The door closed. They were alone. For a full minute, neither of them spoke.

Andie was aware of her own measured breathing; too fast, too loud in the quiet. She cleared her throat just to fill up the silence and returned her attention to the groove in the table. Her fingers resumed picking at the crevice. What was going on? What should she say? Who was this—?

"You don't...remember me?"

"No. Should I?"

"That's right," Tanner said, his voice laced with sarcasm. "The amnesia."

"I don't have to listen to this." Andie climbed to her feet and hurried to the door. She rattled the doorknob but it wouldn't turn.

"What are you doing, Andra?"

Andie looked over her shoulder. "Who?"

"Do you think I'm a complete idiot?" Tanner's voice was barely above a whisper.

"I don't even know you." Andie began pounding on the

door, demanding to be let out.

She heard his chair slide back and turned to face him but he was already there, only inches away. Andie told herself to keep her guard up, along with her chin. But it was impossible to think; his cologne and the soft lull of his voice were beginning to affect her.

Andie backed up to put some space between them but there was nowhere to go. She watched warily as he stepped closer.

He was even more handsome up close. He was a good head taller than Andie, the perfect height to reach up and wrap her arms around his neck and—

She cursed softly as his dark eyes met her own. Where had that thought come from?

"Why don't you just end this little game you're playing and tell me why you did it. "

"Why I did what?"

"Why you left me so long ago. Was this something you and Brian planned together?"

"How do you know Brian?"

Tanner looked at her in disgust. "You know, I came here today thinking maybe we could start over again but these lies—"

"How do you know Brian?"

Tanner tilted his head up, staring at the ceiling. He took a minute before he replied through clenched teeth, "Brian was my bodyguard, as if you didn't know."

"Brian Petersen was my husband."

"Brian Petersen? You mean Brian Phelps?" He lowered his head and stared at her. "And I'm your husband. At least as far as I know." He narrowed his eyes. "Not unless you married after you left me, and that would be against the law."

"Brian and I were already…" Andie looked at the floor in confusion. What was going on? She tried to recall her life before the accident but she ran into a mental road block. What if Brian had been lying to her? That would mean…

This man could be telling the truth.

She turned around, rattling the doorknob again. No. It couldn't be true. This man was mistaken, that was all. She just looked like his wife. They must have misinterpreted her fingerprints. She had heard of it happening before.

Tanner spun her around and pressed her against the wall before she could react. Long, slender fingers curled around her wrists. He brought her hands up, pinning them over her head.

"Look me in the eye and tell me you don't remember me."

"I—I don't." She was going to look away but the flecks of gold in his brown eyes caught her attention—so much like topaz that she couldn't look away.

Tanner pressed his body against hers and lowered his head. His lips were only inches from hers as he whispered, "Is this some kind of punishment for what I did so long ago? Is this to embarrass me, Andra?"

"You're crazy, let me go!" Andie said as his peppermint-laced breath stirred her hair. She squirmed against him and brought her knee up to drive it between his legs but he averted it just in time.

His lips hovered near the corner of hers. "Andra—"

"Let me go, you bastard!" She ripped her head away. "And my name is Andie, not Andra!"

"Did you do it to try to ruin my reputation? Because it only helped me get in office."

Andie relaxed against him. "Are you...are you a politician?"

"I'm the governor of New York. Isn't that what you always wanted?" And then he suddenly laughed. "Look what you've missed all these years. You're probably kicking yourself now for running away, am I right?" He released her hands but didn't step away.

She felt the hardness of his chest through her jumpsuit as he sank against her. He bowed his head, closed his eyes and pressed his forehead against hers. "Look, let's just go home. We can talk about this later."

She closed her eyes as his breath caressed her face.
Governor. He was a governor.

Her head snapped up. After all these years, she was being handed an opportunity of a lifetime. It would mean a different life. Food. A roof over her head. A warm bed. Safety.

No more trying to survive on the streets. No more roaming from shelter to shelter. No more begging for money from the street corner.

This man thought she was his wife. She would play along for a little while. And then she would leave when she got tired of it and maybe take a few mementos with her to remember the occasion.

She lifted her head. "Let's go home."

~ Six ~

His wife was curled in a fetal position, asleep in the seat across from him. Tanner had been warned that she was still recovering from pneumonia and would probably be tired until she fully recovered.

After leaving the police station together even he was surprised by the number of reporters outside. A sea of white news vans lined the street, parked helter-skelter-like for blocks.

Tanner sensed Andra's shock at seeing what awaited her outside. She came to a complete stop on the front steps and would have bolted back inside if Tanner hadn't grasped her hand and led her away from the building. When she saw the limo parked at the curb, she looked over at him and smiled.

It was the first smile he had seen all day. But what awaited him when she awoke?

Andra's arms were crossed defensively even in sleep, her head resting at an uncomfortable angle against the car door. The clothes she wore—baggy jeans and a black sweater so faded it looked gray—were a size too large; either that or she had lost significant weight over the years. Dark circles shadowed her eyes and her hair…

Tanner leaned forward and curled a mahogany strand around his finger. He had never seen it past her shoulders. It now reached the small of her back, a dark, glorious curtain of temptation to any man.

Lowering his hand, Tanner touched her cheek, as if he didn't quite trust what he saw. After ten years, he had finally found her. She was safe.

His gaze traveled over her velvety skin, across her jaw and skimmed her lips. He recalled the harsh words he had spoken to her earlier in the police station and cursed himself for losing his cool. He had entered that room with intentions of making it right between them—but then she had started in with the lies and drama.

Andra had always excelled at both. The police didn't understand that. He had tried explaining her behavior before her disappearance—like the time she had pretended to have an affair just to make him jealous.

Homelessness. Poverty. A criminal record. He believed none of it. It was an act to embarrass him and ruin his reputation.

Tanner sat back, his hand curling into a fist. Would she succeed? What would people think when this story appeared in tomorrow's headlines?

She hadn't changed, even after all these years. Still deceitful and dishonest, just two of the reasons he had threatened divorce. And now? He couldn't go through with divorce now. At least not yet. What would people think? How would it affect his upcoming re-election to divorce a woman he had just found again after ten years?

It would ruin him, worse than her little charade she was trying to pull here.

He couldn't. Not now. He would have to bear with her and try to get through this until after the re-election, which was over a year away. *Could he last that long?*

The privacy glass that separated the front of the limo from the back suddenly whined as it was lowered.

"Sir, we're almost there," Jared said from the front.

"Okay." Tanner looked out the tinted window as the limousine slowed to a stop in front of the hotel.

Tanner lifted his hand to shake Andra awake but hesitated. For selfish reasons, he didn't want to disturb her. If he did, they might start arguing again and he didn't feel up to it this late at night.

Jared climbed out, locked the car doors and entered the hotel. A minute later, he returned with a card key and a room number. He opened Tanner's door. "I think we're all set."

Leaning over, Tanner tucked one hand under Andie's knees, the other around her shoulders.

"Want me to get her?"

"No, I can handle it." As he lifted her from the limousine, Tanner tensed, expecting her to awaken and struggle, but she must have been exhausted because she settled into his arms. He clutched her closer, stepped away from the curb and walked across the sidewalk. Jared retrieved Tanner's luggage from the trunk and hurried ahead of his boss to get the door for him.

Tanner stopped inside the lobby.

Large trees rose to a second story balcony, their branches partially shielding some hotel guests who were leaning against the balcony, overlooking the lobby. Other guests sat in leather furniture, stiff and formal as the room. They looked up at him curiously as he passed by.

On their way to the elevator, they passed open rooms. Tanner glanced inside one of them. Dozens of chairs were set up inside, four to a row in front of a podium used for conferences and seminars. Another appeared to be a formal meeting room, the lights glowing off the rich cherry finish of a table spanning the length of the room.

Jared punched the Up button when they reached the elevators. "I got the penthouse for tonight."

"You didn't have to," Tanner said but knew this was one argument he would lose. As governor, he insisted on saving taxpayers money by getting a standard room when traveling.

Jared always insisted on the penthouse. Better security, he claimed, because there were no neighbors around to worry about. The elevator's doors opened with a whisper. Andie's soft hair brushed his chin as he entered the elevator. Jared followed behind and pressed the button for the penthouse. The elevator whisked them up thirty floors and stopped with a soft ring, announcing its arrival.

The doors opened. Jared brushed past Tanner and scanned the empty hallways before beckoning his boss to leave the safe haven of the elevator.

Tanner waited outside the suite as Jared unlocked it. When the door opened, they were greeted by darkness. Jared entered ahead of him, searching the room before motioning Tanner inside.

Tanner adjusted Andra in his arms as he stepped inside, appalled at her slight weight. She was so tiny, delicately thin. He would order room service immediately and begin putting weight on her bones.

"I'll be right next door if you need me." Jared backed out of the room. "Nobody should bother you. I circled the block several times to shake any reporters who might be tailing us."

"Thanks."

Closing the door, Tanner walked toward the spare bedroom. When Andra murmured in her sleep, she also snuggled against his chest, her arms wrapping tightly around his back, molding herself against him.

Tanner cursed and tried to ignore the way her body curved so perfectly against his. The way her warm, steady breath tickled his throat.

She sighed once again and Tanner felt her stiffen in his arms momentarily before she relaxed once more. Her once-steady breath quickened and he turned to see if she was awake, but her dark cloud of hair shielded her face. Andra's arm slipped off his shoulder and dangled loosely at his side.

As he adjusted her in his arms, he felt...

He stopped walking and tensed as small, nimble fingers touched his back pocket. Tanner almost dropped her when her hand slid gently, easily into his pocket to touch his wallet. The little vixen was pickpocketing him.

Andie opened her eyes as her fingers encountered the wallet bulging in his back pocket. Her mind was no longer fuzzy from sleep. Her senses and defenses had come on full alert when she awoke to find herself cradled against Tanner's chest. She pinched the leather and began to carefully slide it out but she was suddenly dropped.

Andie landed on her feet, agile as a cat. She stepped back but each time she attempted to put distance between them it narrowed as he sauntered toward her.

Bumping into the wall, she looked up as he came close enough for her to see his clenched jaw, darkened from a five o'clock shadow. Andie tensed as his hand tightened into a fist.

She tried to run but his fingers splayed across her shoulders, holding her in place. Crying out, Andie jerked away and bent down, feeling for her switchblade. It wasn't there. The police station had kept it after releasing her into Tanner's custody.

"Let me go!" She fisted her fingers, striking his chest. "Now!"

He stilled her hand. "So you like it rough too, is that it, Andra? That's something new I didn't know about you." Tanner cupped her face and lowered his mouth to hers.

Air drained from Andie's lungs as his lips plundered hers. Strength seeped from her legs as he tugged her hips against the junction of his thighs. Blood emptied from her head as his hands molded her body to his, exploring here, claiming there.

Andie couldn't think. Couldn't react. Her mind fought to reclaim control but her body conquered. She sagged against the wall and moaned, lifting her chin to give him better access to her throat and collarbone.

Tanner dragged his lips to the exposed flesh that she offered and lavished her collarbone, his tongue delving in and out of the smooth valleys.

Andie lifted her hands, entangling her fingers in his hair. This was the cruelest form of punishment. She preferred pain; at least she had been prepared for it. She had experienced it before, both physically and emotionally. But this...this pleasure was new to her.

Her hands betrayed her by sliding down his broad back to settle around his waist.

What had started out as punishment soon softened. Tanner's lips stopped their assault and became more playful, his tongue tracing the contour of her lips, his mouth testing her kisses at each angle.

Andie's mouth opened beneath his, allowing him access. His tongue mated with hers and Tanner matched her groan for groan, gasp for gasp as they—

She jerked away, her heart tripping against her ribcage, and her breath...*she couldn't breathe.*

Andie brought her hands to her face, pressing her palms against her flushed face. What had they done? What had she let him do? *What had she let herself do?* She had fallen into his arms like one of the women who hung out on the street corners.

Her intention had been to share a kiss to distract him while she grabbed his wallet. But all thoughts and intentions had been forgotten when their lips met. And now she had empty pockets to go along with an empty stomach.

Closing his eyes, Tanner bowed his head and dragged air into his starved lungs. It had never been like this before between them. Their kisses had always been cold and passionless. There was no giving and no taking between them, no sharing and no exploring, just two lips meeting in welcome, to bid goodbye, to appear the loving couple in public and to family.

"Are you all right?"

He stiffened. She had never asked that question before. Never seemed concerned enough to voice it.

Tanner stumbled away. His gaze swept up her body. She looked like Andra, sounded like Andra. Yet did not act like her. And most certainly did not kiss like her.

Desire was a powerful, weakening agent and he blamed it for his confusion. He didn't want to feel anything for her.

Turning away, Tanner hurried toward the door.

"Where are you going?"

"Out." He needed to get away. If he stayed any longer, he would fall for her wide-eyed innocent routine. Tanner fumbled with the locks with awkward fingers before he finally managed to turn them and slide off the chain. He yanked open the door. "I'll be back later."

"But where are you going?"

He slammed the door.

~ Seven ~

Andie turned away, kicked off her shoes and studied the room—*she was in a penthouse!* Walking across the ceramic tile of the entryway, she stepped onto plush, shag-like carpet that was so lush she could curl her toes in it. A brown leather sectional couch was centered in the living room, facing a large entertainment center that held a TV, VCR and DVD player. Glass coffee tables flanked the ends of the couch. A leather chair and ottoman stood at attention in the corner of the room. Tall vases dotted nearby tables, filled with plumes of eucalyptus leaves in various colors. Dark, neutral curtains, closed for privacy, adorned each window.

Andie stopped in front of a floor-to-ceiling window and pushed aside the curtains. The city lights of Detroit competed with the stars above.

How had she become so lucky? She whirled around, her eyes sweeping across the room. Her attention was drawn to the kitchenette as the refrigerator hummed to life. A basket sat on the dining room table, filled with crackers, cheese, champagne and chocolate.

She walked across the living room and slowed to grab a chocolate bar from the basket on her way toward the bedrooms. She had to check out the rest of the penthouse to see what other delightful surprises awaited her.

Entering the hallway, she flipped on the light and turned left into one of the two bedrooms. A king-size bed looked miniscule in the large room. The bedspread was turned down for the evening, revealing black satin sheets. Chocolates encased in gold foils rested on both pillows.

She had seen satin bedding in store windows, but how would it feel against her skin?

Another door lay ajar off the bedroom. Andie skirted the bed and reached inside the room, flipping the switch. Bright light splashed the interior of a bathroom, reflecting off the clean tile floor, the marble countertop and gold faucets.

The room smelled like potpourri and a faint scent of disinfectant. She stepped inside and delicately touched the clean, navy blue towels that hung suspended from the towel rack on the wall. The initials of the hotel were embossed in white. Rubbing the material between her thumb and forefinger, she realized they were softer than anything she had ever felt before.

She pulled a towel off the rack, burying her face in it. Andie inhaled the clean detergent scent. She had never used blue towels before. Not that she could recall. The only towels she had used were the homeless shelter's thin, white, frayed towels that people had donated.

A basket rested in the corner of the large tub, which held shampoo, conditioner and bubble bath. She uncapped the bath bubbles and inhaled. Vanilla.

She clutched the bottle to her chest and glanced again at the tub. She couldn't remember ever being in a bathtub. The homeless shelter offered only community showers, and her modesty forced her to use them only in the dead of night when everyone was asleep. And quickly too, for fear that a man might walk in to sneak a peek.

Shutting the bathroom door, Andie stripped off her clothes. She would make this quick before Tanner returned.

Leaning over, she turned on the water and adjusted the temperature. She tapped a few drops of vanilla bath bubbles into the water and then greedily dumped the whole bottle in. She felt almost giddy as the bubbles thickened and white foam settled on top.

Looking into the mirror, she caught herself grinning. At the police station, Tanner had seemed surprised by her sudden change in attitude. If he only knew what she'd experienced—and what she had not—these past ten years, he would understand why she so suddenly agreed to go with him.

She had it good now. How many people could say they had stayed the night in a penthouse suite?

She stepped into the water and slipped beneath the bubbles. As the heady scent of vanilla enveloped her, Andie closed her eyes and relaxed. She released a soft sigh of pleasure as she rested her head against the wall but then straightened and began soaping up when she remembered her time limit. Tanner would be back soon.

Andie quickly worked shampoo into her hair and wondered if she shouldn't be so strict with herself. Maybe she could take a few minutes to—

The front door opened and closed.

"Andra!" Tanner called from the living room.

Andie stiffened. He had returned sooner than expected. Afraid to turn on the faucet for fear that he would hear, Andie bent over and furiously tried to splash water on her hair to rinse the shampoo. But her hair was too long and there was too much shampoo in it.

"Andra! Where are you?" His voice was much clearer, closer this time.

Andie wiped bubbles off her forehead but only succeeded in splashing shampoo into her eyes. She cried out as it began to sting. Rubbing her eyes with one hand, she reached out with the other and felt for the towel but it was not within reach.

"Andra?"

He was right outside the door!

Andie cried out in frustration as her blind search turned

up nothing. She could see nothing and had to get the shampoo out of her eyes before he—
        The door opened.

~ Eight ~

"Andra?"
        She slid deeper into the bubbles to shield her body. But it was too late. Tanner saw everything from the waist up. And what a sight it had been, too. Pale, creamy skin, full breasts, silky hair. Tanner closed his mouth when he realized he was gawking like a teenager.
        He sucked in a deep breath. Told himself to back out of the room and give her some privacy, but he couldn't move. Gone was the dirt and ugly clothing, and in its place was a beautiful woman.
        She had committed a sin by hiding that body under such drab clothing. This woman deserved elegant gowns and jewelry. Tanner's gaze followed the curve of her neck and stopped on her bowed head. But even those items would pale next to her.
        His eyebrows drew together when he realized she wouldn't look at him. Her hands covered her face. Was she embarrassed? When he heard her sniff, concern replaced desire.
        Tanner sank to his knees beside the whirlpool. "Andra? Are you all right?" He touched a wet tendril of hair and discovered it was as silky as it looked. "Are you hurt?"
        "Please…just leave." Andie tensed when Tanner's hands touched her hair and trailed down the curve of her jaw. Were all crucial parts of her anatomy concealed? *And just how much had he seen when he walked through the door?*
        "I can't see. I have shampoo in my eyes." Andie brought her knees against her chest to shield her body. "Can you hand me a towel?"
        Her movement only succeeded in revealing more of her body. Bubbles cascaded down her bare legs and slipped into

the water. Tanner closed his eyes briefly but the image was embedded in his memory.

He tried to take another deep breath but couldn't. What air he did manage to drag into his lungs didn't last long when she shifted, exposing her hip.

Tanner realized he was staring and ripped his gaze back to her face. Andra could be hurt or in pain and this was how he responded? By making love to her body with his eyes? Imagining what her soft skin would feel like? Wondering how she would respond under him?

"Uh...what?"

"A towel. *Please.*"

Tanner reached forward, ripped the towel off the rack and slid closer. He tried to help but she batted his hands away.

"I can do it," she insisted.

Tanner dampened a corner of the towel with fresh water from the faucet. "Your hands are covered with suds. You'll only get more in your eyes if you try. Let me help."

Andie wanted to hate him for embarrassing her, but when she felt his cool hands delicately cup her face and press a wet towel against her closed eyes, her anger disappeared.

She preferred Tanner's cold, suspicious looks, his scowls and temper. This concern he exhibited was something to be avoided because she might succumb to it, might even end up liking him.

She heard his quick intake of breath and felt her nipples pucker. Her breasts were exposed. Gasping, she slid deeper into the water, cursing softly for not filling the tub more.

Tanner blinked and licked his dry lips. The scent of vanilla assaulted his nostrils. He leaned closer and inhaled, feeling his body respond to it. To her.

He wanted to lift her from the water and carry her to his bed. Would she be as feisty and passionate in bed as she was out of it?

Tanner's thoughts stilled along with his rapid breathing when he saw her shoulders trembling. It wasn't cold in the room; the glaring lights and humidity wouldn't permit it. It could only mean one thing—she was frightened. And that thought sapped all desire from his body. She didn't trust him. And right then, he didn't trust himself, so he stood up and backed away.

He wrung the towel nervously. "Better?"

Andie cracked her eyes open and blinked. "Yes. Thank you." She crossed her arms over her chest and lowered her eyes. Why didn't she tell him to get out? She had never hesitated to voice her thoughts before, so why now?

It was because she was naked, she thought. When she had stripped off her clothing, another part of herself had been peeled away and discarded: her confidence and boldness. She was vulnerable.

Tanner's eyes drifted to the hair that lay thick, wet, and curled around her shoulders. He wanted to plunge his hands in it and bring it to his face to inhale the sweet scent but clenched his fists to still the impulse. He should leave now.

Tanner retreated. "Do you need anything else?"

"No. I can manage."

"I'll go check on room service. It should be here any minute."

"Okay."

Tanner shut the door and sagged against it. He closed his eyes as water splashed from inside the bathroom. He imagined her rising out of the water like a siren from the sea, bath bubbles cascading down her body. Envisioned her long legs stepping onto the floor, the plush towel pressing against her body as she dried herself.

She might not need anything else at the moment, Tanner thought, but he most certainly did—a cold shower.

~~~~

Andie didn't want to leave the safe haven of the bathroom. How could she face Tanner after what had happened?

She found a robe hanging on the back of the door and cinched its belt around her waist. It covered her from shoulders to ankles but it wasn't enough to shield her body from Tanner's probing eyes as he looked up in the middle of pouring a glass of champagne.

"So what do you think about the suite?"

Her shoulder lifted in a shrug. "It's all right." She didn't want to encourage a conversation. If she did, she might begin to feel more comfortable around him.

"How are you feeling? I heard you were getting over pneumonia."

"I feel much better."

"There's some new clothes, makeup and other stuff in your room if you want to change after dinner. I hope they're okay."

"What do you mean?"

"Jared bought them," he replied. "Normally I'd have one of my female assistants shop for you but Jared's the only one traveling with me this time. We could have gone out to shop around but reporters are all over outside."

"I'm sure they'll be fine." Andie crossed to the window and pushed aside the curtain to look outside but it was too dark to see anything below.

"Trust me. They're out there. They were like a dog with a bone when they heard that you'd been found." Tanner pulled a chair out from the table. "Why don't you sit down, Andra? I had Jared go out and buy some of your favorite champagne."

"My name is Andie." She looked down at the food. Succulent chicken breasts covered in thick gravy. Potatoes. Carrots. Biscuits. And a cherry cheesecake for dessert. Her mouth began watering from the smell. She had never seen so much food before.

"Is—is all that for me?" Andie drifted to the table and sat across from him, pulling her chair closer. She grabbed her fork and knife and sliced the chicken quickly, as if he would change his mind and take it away. She stuffed her mouth with forkfuls of meat, chewing, swallowing, reaching for more.

Tanner lowered his fork, smiling. "Do you even taste that?" Andie closed her eyes and sighed in content as she chewed. Delicious. She ate mostly soups and sandwiches from the shelters, whatever cheap meal people had donated that day. Chicken was a rarity.

She eyed the piece of cherry cheesecake, a true delicacy rarely offered. Reaching for a piece, Andie snatched it off the plate, holding the other hand under it to catch any crumbs.

Tanner glanced down at her fork. "Aren't you going to use a fork?"

Andie clutched it possessively against her chest. She'd had her food taken away too many times in the past. "I'm not sharing, if that's what you're hinting at."

He offered her his clean fork. "Would you like a fork?"

As a silent rebuff, she brought the cheesecake to her mouth, sinking her teeth into it. Tanner watched as her tongue darted out to lick her lips. Andie closed her eyes, a look of pleasure softening her face as she held the cherry taste on her tongue.

This is how she would look while making love, Tanner thought, as his body went from a dull ache to full-blown agony. He squirmed in the cushioned chair but couldn't shift his eyes from the source of pain. She was too interesting to watch. He never thought a simple act like eating could be so enjoyable, but Andie found it to be. She treasured every bite as if it would be her last.

Cherry glaze smeared the corner of her mouth. He wanted to kiss it off but didn't want to frighten her. So he let his finger mimic what his lips wanted to do, and gently dabbed it away.

Andie closed her eyes at the cool touch of his fingertip. She was tempted to turn her face against his hand and kiss his palm.

She bolted to her feet and found her legs as weak as her breath. What was *wrong* with her? Where had that thought come from? Didn't she remember Brian? The men on the streets who thought she was a streetwalker and treated her like one?

Andie wanted to walk away until she could get her thoughts and breath in tight control.

Tanner eased back in his chair. "Are you okay?"

"Yes."

"Why don't you come back to the table?"

She returned to her chair and sat down.

He poured her a glass of champagne. "Try some."

She brought it to her lips and swallowed, grimacing at the bitter taste. Lowering the glass, she pushed it away. "That stuff is terrible!"

"It was your favorite."

More proof that she wasn't his wife, Andie thought, refilling her water.

He slid the champagne bottle back in the ice bucket and stood up. "I'll be right back." He disappeared into his bedroom and returned a minute later, a manila folder and picture album clutched under his arm.

"I brought these along with me just in case I'd need them." He picked the chair closest to her and sat down.

"What is it?" She leaned over to look and tensed as she accidentally brushed against him. Andie glanced up, noticing for the first time that his hair was wet from a shower. His face was freshly shaven. The scent of shampoo mixed with aftershave made her inhale deeply before she realized what she was doing.

She straightened suddenly as he opened the manila folder, revealing news clippings.

"I've saved these over the years." He spread them across the table. They were all about his missing wife. She peered closer at the picture of Andra Thornburg and gasped before she could contain it.

"What is it?"

"She looks like me."

"You are her."

"No, she just *looks* like me."

"You really don't believe you're my wife?" Tanner

pushed it toward Andie. "Here, look. These are our wedding pictures."

She flipped through the album. Tanner and his wife exchanging vows. Tanner and his wife lighting the unity candle. Slipping on the rings.

Peering closer, she looked at the woman's face. It was uncanny. Could it be her? Why wouldn't she remember her wedding day? Andie looked up and met Tanner's eyes. Why wouldn't she remember her husband?

"But Brian—"

"Brian kidnapped you, Andra...Andie. He only posed as your husband."

Glancing down at the picture, Andie thought how much she resembled the woman in the picture. Her hair was a lot shorter in the picture and her eyes...they looked different. More narrowed, more – *the word didn't come to her right away*—shrew-like, she realized.

Andie closed the book. "It can't be me."

"How can you say that? You're the spitting image of her."

"These pictures are old and taken from a distance."

"What more proof do you need to believe you are Andra Thornburg? Your fingerprints match. I brought the clippings, the pictures. I bet you even have her birthmark."

"Birthmark?"

"A birthmark on your ankle."

Andie stiffened. How had he known about that?

"Well? Am I right?"

Andie clenched her jaw but said nothing.

Tanner turned toward her and leaned over, grabbing her leg and lifting it for his inspection.

"Cut that out!"

His fingers were surprisingly soft as he lifted her leg and gently twisted it to see the small birthmark. Lowering his hand, he touched it briefly as if he didn't quite believe it was there.

A dozen protests filled Andie's mind and she was about to voice them when his inquisitive touch turned into a caress.

His hand curled around her leg and cupped her calf as his other hand began trailing soft, butterfly-like strokes up and down her legs until a warm liquid began pooling in her feminine parts.

"I wish it could have been different between us. I wish—"

"Things were bad?"

He nodded as she lowered her leg and tried to collect her scattered thoughts. *It was true.* She was his long-lost wife. She'd be foolish not to believe it now, after all this proof.

He had been telling the truth. What would this mean now? How could she use him, deceive him like she intended?

She couldn't, not after all he'd been through. The poor man had been searching for her for *ten years.* What had he suffered during that time?

"How long were we married before I disappeared?"

"Two years."

"Do we have children?"

"No."

"How did we meet?"

"Through your father," Tanner replied.

"I have a father?"

"He was a senator from New York."

Her father, a senator? How could she not remember? It was like they were talking about someone other her.

"He passed away about a year after you were taken," Tanner said. "Collapsed from a heart attack. I guess it was too much for him."

"And my mother?"

"Died a few years before from breast cancer."

She sat silently, reflecting on what her life must have been like before Brian had taken her. She'd been cheated out of her own life. She'd had people who had loved her. She'd lived a pampered, privileged life.

Andie pushed herself to her feet, suddenly exhausted from the rollercoaster of emotions.

"Andra, are you okay?"

"This is a lot to take in. I just need some time to myself."

"Is there anything I can do?"

She shook her head and hurried to her bedroom, sagging against the closed door before her legs collapsed at the thought of what she had lost so long ago—her identity, her husband, her parents, and life as she'd known it.

~ Nine ~

That night after she heard Tanner retire to his bedroom, Andie opened the French doors and stepped onto the private balcony outside her bedroom. She shut the doors softly behind her and crossed to the railing.

It had begun snowing. Snowflakes whipped her face. A layer was beginning to form on the balcony. If she listened very carefully, she could hear Christmas music on the streets below.

It was almost December. She had always looked forward to this time of year. December was the month for giving. The only month where handouts were plentiful. Homeless shelters handed out baskets of clothes and food during this season. Then it all slowed down to a trickle again after the New Year.

She gripped the railing until her knuckles paled. She didn't fit into Tanner's world. He didn't fit into hers. He was a governor. He was respected for his money and title. Tanner probably knew nothing about hunger pangs, fright, or worrying about where to get his next meal.

Andie remembered the shared kiss and the vulnerable feelings it invoked. What was she doing? Why was she doing this? She thought she could keep her distance but he was making it difficult.

He was too kind. And definitely too handsome.

Andie was beginning to like him, which was why she couldn't stay. No amount of money would be worth subjecting herself to weakness and vulnerability. She refused to be at the mercy of a man—any man—again. Even if he was New York's governor.

Releasing her grip on the railing, Andie returned to her bedroom. She flung open the closet doors. Several sweaters hung inside, price tags still dangling from the sleeves. She fingered the bright red fabric of one. She'd never felt anything like it before. Lifting the tag inside the collar, she saw that it was made from something called angora. She slipped it on over her head and turned around, pulling open dresser drawers until she found jeans folded inside.

Changing quickly, she stepped into the hall. Paused outside Tanner's door. Listened. Nothing from inside.

She crossed the living room and hesitated at the front door. She took a deep breath, turned the doorknob and—

"Going somewhere?"

Andie spun around as Tanner's soft voice penetrated the darkness. She peered into the shadowed room and saw him lounging on a kitchen barstool with a drink clenched in his hand.

"Oh! I—I didn't see you there. I thought I heard you go to bed. What are you doing up?"

Tanner flipped on the kitchen light, revealing a bottle of whiskey on the counter. "Call me Tanner. Please." Reaching for the bottle, he filled his glass with the amber liquid. "And I was about to ask you the same thing."

Andie looked around the room for an excuse, something she could say to ease the suspicion in his eyes. Something—

The piano. An ivory grand piano rested in the corner of the living room. Only the black keys distinguished it from the ivory rug and walls. It was more for show but it was beautiful and a shame that the heavy lid was closed, locking away the music trapped inside.

"Are you trying to escape?"

"I'm not a criminal! Don't treat me like one!"

"Then what are you doing up at this hour?" Tanner glanced at the grandfather clock. "It's almost two in the morning."

"If you must know, I couldn't sleep so I thought I'd come out and play the piano," she said, pleased that the lie came out so smoothly.

Tanner followed her gaze to the piano. "Be my guest." He swept his hand toward the piano. "I'd love to listen." "Uh...that's all right. It's late and I'm sure you're tired." Tanner smiled lazily as his eyes wandered down her body. "On the other hand, I can think of another kind of music we can make together that has nothing to do with pianos." She narrowed her eyes. "You're drunk." He shrugged and brought his glass to his mouth, watching her from over the golden rim of liquor. "I'm giving you the choice, Andie. Which kind of music would you like? And where would you like to play? Here, in the living room?" His eyes traveled up her body and paused on her breasts. "Or in the bedroom?"

His shirt was unbuttoned, as if he had been getting ready for bed but had changed his mind at the last minute. Andie tried to look away but her eyes were drawn to the mat of dark chest hair, which raced down to circle his navel before tapering to a thin line into his—

Andie looked away as a blush settled in her cheeks.

"I love music," Tanner said. "Please."

Andie didn't remember walking over to the piano but blinked and found herself standing before it, gazing down at it like she didn't quite know what to make of it.

Tanner laughed. "It won't bite, you know."

She lifted the top of the piano bench and found it empty. "I can't play if I don't have music." This was the excuse she would need to get him off her back, she thought, dropping the bench lid loudly. Now he would end his torment.

"You must know something."

Sinking on the piano bench, Andie sighed as she swung her legs over. Lifting her hands, she swept them lightly over the ivory keys, feeling them give beneath her hand. Andie closed her eyes and rested her hands on the keys.

And then she began to play.

Notes turned into music, music turned into a melody, and the melody turned into a song. *How was that possible?*

Her foot tapped the pedal below, changing the music from mellow to dramatic, dramatic to mellow. Her hands flew over the keys as music drifted from the inner core of the piano. She had heard this song somewhere before, but where? A scene unfolded in her mind, her first full memory in years. She was dressed in an emerald green evening gown, sitting before a piano, singing softly and turning the pages of sheet music. A large floor-to-ceiling Christmas tree was beside the piano, the lights glowing off the piano's sheen. People were standing around, listening intently to the music.

Andie was so lost in the music and the remembrance that she didn't see him slip off the barstool and wander across the room. Didn't sense him standing behind her.

But her concentration finally broke when his hands settled on her shoulders. He leaned over, his breath stirring her hair as he whispered, "That's *Moonlight Sonata*. It was your favorite song. Can you remember anything else?"

Andie stopped playing, silencing the music in mid-song. The drumming of her heartbeat took up the rhythm where her hands left off.

She closed her eyes and tried to mentally grasp the scene but it drifted away like the fading notes of the song.

"Do you remember when I used to do this?" Tanner's lips touched the back of her neck, so soft she thought she had imagined it. "Or this?" His tongue circled each delicate bone in the back of her neck. His hands settled around her waist, erotically stroking her hip.

His feathered kisses sent shivers darting up and down Andie's back before settling warmly in places she didn't even know she had.

Andie turned around on the bench, opening her arms and legs to him. Tanner responded to her silent invitation by sinking to his knees. He pushed away her hair and ran his thumb across the arch of her eyebrow before lowering it to brush over her parted lips.

"You are so beautiful."

Andie wanted to open her mouth against his finger and draw it into her mouth to taste the sweet whiskey she could smell on his hand. She bit her lip. What would he think of her if she did something like that?

He would think she had taken more from men than just their wallets.

Tanner smoothed her frown away with his finger, and when that didn't work, he used his mouth. He cupped her face and rained petal-soft kisses on her lips, her cheeks, her eyebrows. He was so gentle; nobody had ever treated her this way before.

Tanner's hand drifted down to curl around her throat. His thumb caressed her pulse, creating eddies of warmth through her body. He drew away to whisper, "Andie, you're so beautiful...I want to...oh God..." before his tongue parted her lips and came to the barrier of her teeth. He groaned as she opened her mouth to his. He dipped inside, tasting the sweet recesses of her mouth, plunging, receding, plunging, receding, each time dragging moans from her mouth.

Andie lifted her arms and wound them around his neck, burying her fingers into the soft black curls. She moaned as his tongue withdrew to trace the contour of her lips.

Tanner moved closer until his groin was nestled between her legs. As the soft cotton trousers touched her thighs, Andie stiffened. Tanner seemed to sense her hesitation and lifted his mouth.

"Andie, I won't hurt you. I'll never hurt you. Never." His tongue darted in her ear to explore the curves. His fingertips soothingly stroked up and down her thighs until she relaxed against him.

And then he slowly sank against her. His chest rose and fell, competing with hers. His mouth claimed the hollow of her throat and ventured over her collarbone. Her nipples swelled and tightened and a dull ache began flaring in a place she had never ached before.

Tanner picked her up and set her gently on the ivory keys, the piano squawking in protest under her slight weight. Her heart jack hammered and she was certain he could feel it. She wanted him to feel it. Wanted him to lift his hand and press it against her heart, mold it around her left breast.

"Tanner." She had meant it as a protest but it came out as a breathless sigh.

His sigh matched hers as he pushed away her hair, trailing his finger over the red path his stubble had created on the sensitive skin of her throat. And then his mouth replaced his finger as he kissed away the blaze.

"Tanner!" Andie lifted her hands and Tanner pulled his mouth away and opened his eyes, expecting her to push him away. Or slap him. But she did neither. She lowered her hands to his head and caressed his hair, writhing under him in a silent plea for more.

The memory of that night with Brian returned, which still haunted her to this day. Sitting up, Andie pushed him away. *"No, stop!"*

"What is it? Did I hurt you?"

Andie touched her swollen whiskey-laced lips, remembering that night so long ago. Brian had kissed her with the same taste of whiskey on his lips. Afterward, she had also had swollen lips, but not from his kisses.

"Brian…"

Fury filled Tanner's face as he ground out through clenched teeth, "Did he hurt you, Andie?"

Andie lifted her eyes and met his, but no longer were they filled with terror. They were wide, defeated, glazed over, as if she were lost in another time and place.

Tanner reached out to comfort her, but Andie shied away like a startled horse.

"Andie, I'm not going to hurt you. I'll never hurt you. Please, just let me hold you."

"Get away from me!"

"Did Brian hurt you, baby?" He lifted his hands slowly, carefully, and placed them on her shoulders. What he wanted to do was wrap her in his arms and not let go until she stopped shivering. "Did he…did he…"

He couldn't say it. Didn't want to think it. Couldn't even imagine it. But he forced it up his throat and stammered, "Did—did Brian…rape you, Andie?" Tanner clenched his jaw, along with his fists. If he had, Tanner would raise the amount of reward money for Brian's capture. He would send posters around the world until he found his former bodyguard.

And then he would deal with Brian Phelps himself.

"No, but he tried." Andie collapsed on the floor and brought her knees against her chest. She covered her face with trembling hands, trying to control the hot rush of tears that welled in her eyes and threatened to spill down her cheeks.

She had never cried in front of a man since Brian. She couldn't now. He would think she was weak, nothing but a simpering female.

Tanner fell to his knees and wrapped his arms around her, rocking her, soothing her, kissing her hair. Instead of fighting him, Andie buried her face against his chest, craving the security his arms offered.

And only then did she release the tears she had dammed up for ten years.

~ Ten ~

In two days, Andra would be home. It still sounded so strange to Tanner. Andra. *Home.*

Ten years ago, his hope of finding her had faded as a week passed, a month, a year. He thought he would never see her again.

He had already called his assistant and explained why he couldn't return home to Albany for some time. He couldn't thrust Andra into that lifestyle yet.

They would return to the penthouse; it was where Andra had grown up. Perhaps her memory would return if she was in a familiar place.

Any work would be done from his office in New York City, he thought.

Tanner paced the living room of the suite, hands clasped behind his back. He wanted to do something special for her homecoming. But what? A party? No, that was out of the question. It was too soon to thrust her into that spotlight.

He had already made arrangements to have a room prepared for her. His assistant had bought Andra necessities like new clothing and personal items.

What would she think of the return home? Would she like it? *Would she stay?*

That was the question Tanner worried about most. She had already tried one escape attempt. Would she try again? And most disturbingly, would he stop her if she did?

If she wanted to go badly enough, there was nothing he could do to stop her.

Tanner stopped pacing when he heard the shower stop. She had been in there a long time—he glanced at the clock—nearly thirty minutes. What had she been doing?

An image of her primping for him came to mind but he immediately discarded it. He felt guilty about what had nearly happened last night. It was too soon to expect them to be husband and wife again in every way.

He sat next to the phone and pulled it closer. Reaching for the phone book, he looked up a local flower shop and dialed.

"Scents of Time, may I help you?"

"Yes, I'd like to have some flowers delivered, please. To New York."

"Yes, sir, may I have your name, sir?"

The woman asked several more questions about the delivery. Several fall-colored flower arrangements would arrive at the penthouse in the next few days. He would have to call home to have them placed throughout her bedroom as a surprise.

As the woman on the phone totaled the amount, he glanced at his watch. They had fifteen minutes to get to the restaurant before their reservations were given to somebody else. "Your total comes to ninety-three dollars even, Mr. Thornburg. Will this be on a Visa or MasterCard today, sir?" Tanner reached for his wallet and flipped it open. "Visa." He scanned his credit cards. Marshall Fields. Discover. *Where was his Visa?*

"Uh, umm, just a minute, please," Tanner mumbled.

He trailed his fingers down the row of credit cards wedged in the leather folds of his wallet. Had he given Jared his Visa card earlier that night instead? No, he was quite sure he had given him the MasterCard to buy the champagne.

Both were missing.

He flipped the leather wallet closed.

"Mr. Thornburg, sir?"

"Yes, I'm still here. I'm having...difficulty finding the right credit card."

"Oh." Her voice dipped, as if she didn't believe him.

Tanner clenched his jaw. "I guess I'll have to call back later when I find my cards, ma'am."

"We'll keep your order on file, sir," she said, giving him an order number. "Just give that number the next time you call and we won't have to go through this all over again."

"Thank you, ma'am," he whispered before hanging up.

The bathroom door cracked open and Andra emerged, dressed in jeans. She pulled a comb through her hair as she walked down the hallway toward him.

Tanner lifted his head. Andra. Had she taken the credit card when he wasn't looking? She tried to pick his pocket the first night they had arrived at the hotel. What would stop her from trying again?

Tanner climbed slowly to his feet.

"Tanner, I'm not sure I'm up to going out tonight," she said as she entered the living room. "I'm not—"

The murderous look on his face must have stopped her because she looked up at him with narrowed her eyes. "What?"

He held out his hand. "Where is it?"

"Where is what?"

"You know what!"

She lowered the hand that gripped the comb. "No. I don't know what."

"I was beginning to trust you, Andra, and you go ahead and do this to me!"

"Do what?"

Tanner lowered his hand and turned away, loosening the tie he had so carefully worked on. Unable to untie it, her pulled it over his head and flung it on the couch. Reaching for his belt buckle, he ripped his belt off and tossed that on the couch too.

Her eyes widened. "What are you doing?"

"I'm changing! What the hell does it look like I'm doing?" Tanner walked into his bedroom and reached for a pair of jeans.

She followed him inside. "What's wrong? Aren't we going out tonight?"

"Not now!"

"What happened from the time I stepped into the bathroom until the time I got out?"

Tanner glared at her over his shoulder as he unzipped his pants and slipped them off. He crossed the room, clad only in his boxers and an unbuttoned dress shirt, both of which quickly followed his trousers to the floor before being replaced by a New York Rangers T-shirt. He slipped his jeans on and buttoned them up. He then strode toward her and watched as she backed up and hit the wall, nowhere to go. He advanced. She tried to skirt away from him but he grasped her elbow and used his body to pin her against the wall.

He lifted his hands and pressed them against the wall on either side of her head. Leaning down, he said, "Where is it?"

"Where is what?"

"My credit card! It's gone!"

"Well, I didn't take it!"

"Nobody else could have! And nobody around here has

the criminal record you do!"

"You don't trust me."

"Why should I? You've given me no reason to," he said.

"You tried taking my wallet the first night here. Remember?" She tried to push him away but he was like a wall. "Get away from me."

"Not until you give me my credit card. I know you have it."

"I don't have it!"

"I was going to treat you to dinner and flowers and this is how you thank me?"

"How many times do I have to tell you, I don't have it!"

He lowered his hands and slipped one into the back pocket of her jeans, cupping her rear end through the denim fabric.

"What are you doing?"

His hand delved into her front pocket. "Looking for my credit card."

She tried to bat his hand away. "Stop it, Tanner!"

The door burst open and Tanner straightened, looking over his shoulder at Jared who stood in the doorway. His face flamed red when he saw what they were doing.

"I'm sorry, sir. I tried knocking a few times but nobody was answering." He started to close the door but Tanner broke away and crossed the room toward his bodyguard.

"Jared, you didn't take my Visa card, did you?"

"Uh, sir?"

"My Visa card," he said in frustration. "You haven't seen it or taken it, have you?"

He lowered his hand to his wallet and slipped it from his back pocket. He withdrew a credit card. "You mean this?"

"No, that's my MasterCard. Have you seen my…" Tanner looked closer.

Jared looked at the card. "This is your Visa card, Governor."

He opened his lips but nothing came out. "But I thought…I mean, I could have sworn I…" He walked back into his bedroom and grabbed his pants off the floor. Opening his wallet, he pulled out every credit card. Each one fell on the bed.

Including the MasterCard.

He studied the card lying on the bed. He looked up at Andra. "It must have got stuck behind another card."

"Sir?" Jared asked from the doorway. "Was I not supposed to take this card? This is the one you gave me to buy the champagne."

Tanner began picking up the credit cards. "No, it was my mistake."

Jared returned the card to him and closed the door, leaving them alone.

Tanner turned around and faced Andra. "I'm sorry. I must have—"

She hurried toward her room and turned to close the door but he barged in behind her.

"Get out!"

"Andra…Andie, I know you must be mad and I'm sorry I—"

"You accused me of stealing your credit card!"

"I know, and I'm sorry. But given your background, I just thought—"

"You thought wrong!"

"How can you blame me? You have a criminal record."

"You didn't trust me!"

"You've tried taking my wallet before!"

Andra spread her feet and crossed her arms. "Please leave."

Tanner lifted his hands and settled them gently on her shoulder. "I'm very sorry."

"You hurt my feelings."

"I know," he said, lifting his hand to her face. He dragged his fingers across her lips before lowering his hand to her throat, feeling her swallow nervously under his fingertips. "I'm sorry. Do you forgive me?"

She met his eyes and nodded.

His thumb traveled over the arch of her eyebrow. "There is one good thing that came out of all this, though."

"Yeah, what's that?" She closed her eyes briefly as his fingertips fluttered briefly over her eyes before returning to her shoulders.

"I trust you now more than I ever did before."

She opened her eyes. "I won't steal from you."

"I know that now," he lowered his hand to grasp hers. "Let's order in tonight instead, what do you say?"

~ Eleven ~

"Where are you going?" Andie squinted at Tanner in the glare of the bathroom lights.

Tanner glanced at Andie in the mirror. She had just woken up, as evidenced by her sleep-tousled hair and husky morning voice.

He slipped a tie around his neck and buttoned the collar flaps. "I have a press conference downstairs. I need to make a statement about what happened."

Andie watched him fumble with his tie before stepping inside the bathroom. She edged around him until she was facing him. "For a man who wears ties a lot, you sure are making a mess out of that." She lifted her hands and began expertly tying the knot like she did it every day.

Andie straightened the knot, her hands lingering a bit too long. Where had she learned to tie a man's tie? She closed her eyes when a memory from long ago suddenly emerged from a long-dormant mind.

Tanner had just graduated with a law degree. They'd been dating a little over four months and were getting ready to visit her parents. Tanner was about to meet the wealthy Livingston's for the first time. He'd been so nervous that she'd had to tie his tie for him.

"Andie? You okay?"

"I just remembered something. That's all."

He curled his fingers around her wrists. "What did you remember?"

"You. Us. Before we were married. We were in my

apartment, getting ready to meet my parents."

"I remember."

"You're as nervous now as you were then."

"Who says I'm nervous?"

"Is it because of my background? Are you nervous that it'll come out?"

He looked in the mirror as he straightened his tie. "Of course not."

"You're embarrassed, aren't you? That's why you're nervous—because you'll have to explain everything."

"I'm not ashamed of you. And the public won't be either. They'll understand."

"Do you want me to go with you down there?"

Tanner shook his head. "No, stay here. It shouldn't take too long."

~~~~~

As Andie waited on hold, she watched the press conference live on TV. Tanner stood behind the podium as if he belonged there, looking every bit the governor he was. His hands clutched the sides of the podium as he carefully explained the situation surrounding his wife's sudden appearance and then patiently answered reporter's questions.

He had mentioned nothing about her past. Nothing about her record. And she wondered what would happen when he did. What would people think of her? More importantly, what would people think of him? Would they be supportive, knowing that their governor's wife had a criminal record?

They would turn on him. His opponents would have a field day. She was sure of it. And she couldn't put him through that. That's why she couldn't stay.

Andie twirled the phone cord around her index finger as she listened to the music drone on the other end. She glanced at the clock. She'd been on hold for nearly ten minutes. Tanner would be wrapping up the press conference soon and making his way up—

"Hello, ma'am? I'm sorry for making you wait," said the woman at the front desk. "We were able to arrange a shuttle for you but it won't be here for another ten minutes. Is that okay?"

"That's fine."

"The shuttle will be waiting for you in the parking ramp," the woman said. "I already have your credit card number and all necessary information so you're free to leave when it arrives."

"Thanks again." Andie hung up.

From Tanner's bed, she stood and dropped his credit card on the night stand, where he would be sure to find it. She had taken it from his wallet that morning while he was in the shower. Lifting a hand, she squeezed the bridge of her nose. She had never felt guilt before. It ate at her, worse than the headache between her eyes. But was it guilt over taking the card? Or leaving Tanner? And should she take it with her now?

She gazed at the card. No. She had done enough damage. She would manage on her own; she always had. She left it on the bedside table, crossed the hallway and entered her own room to pack what little belongings she had.

She had to leave, return to her old life, and manage to find a stable job and a roof over her head. And somehow forget these past few days with Tanner.

She slung her bag over her shoulder and opened the front door, looking for security. Stepping into the hallway, she peeked around the corner and saw Jared McPherson walk away as he patrolled the hallway.

Earlier, she'd overheard Tanner and Jared arguing as Tanner was leaving to go downstairs. Jared had insisted on accompanying him downstairs. Tanner insisted he stay behind.

To watch *over* Andie? she wondered. Or *watch* Andie?

Tanner had obviously won.

She shut the door quietly and hurried toward the elevator, punching the button.

"Come on, come on!" She talked quietly to herself while she watched the numbers above the door as the elevator made a slow ascent to the penthouse.

The elevator *dinged* open, the noise sharp in the quiet. Andie hurried inside and held her breath as she waited for the doors to close. Her hand bypassed the button for the lobby and went to the one below it, Parking. The elevator began its descent. She held her breath as it stopped at the lobby.

Oh no. Andie's eyes widened as the door opened, revealing an elderly couple. She backed into the corner as they struggled to roll their suitcases inside. Curious hotel staff members and reporters mingled in the lobby. Only one would have to look up and recognize her to ruin her chance at escape. She lowered her head, allowing her hair to shield her face as a cameraman from Fox News walked by, his camera perched on his shoulder.

"Get a shot of the governor coming out," someone said to the cameraman as he swung his camera around.

"There he is!"

A flurry of reporters, too late that morning to squeeze into the conference room, pushed forward, trying to get closer to the governor. Andie leaned forward and helped the elderly man with his luggage.

"Governor! Governor Thornburg, just a few more questions!"

"No more questions," Tanner said. "I've already made my statement."

She had to get out of here. She punched the button to close the elevator doors and the elevator jerked to life again, descending to the underground parking ramp.

The elderly woman stared hard at her. Andie broke eye contact but the woman said,

"You look like her, like the governor's wife. The one they found a few days ago, after being gone so long."

Andie smiled stiffly. "I get that a lot."

The elevator shuddered to a stop. The doors opened. Andie waited while the couple gathered their luggage and exited the elevator. She stepped out and glanced down at the watch Tanner had Jared buy for her. Fifteen minutes had passed since she had called for a shuttle. It should be here by now.

When it still hadn't arrived five minutes later, she began getting nervous. What if Tanner had already found her missing and—

An empty soda can skittered across the pavement. It appeared in front of a car, still spinning on its side, wound to a halt and remained still. Andie held her breath and glanced around, aware of the quiet.

She was alone. The elderly couple had left a few minutes ago.

Probably the wind, she thought. She backed against the wall and scanned the darkness. They really needed more lighting down here. It wasn't safe. Anybody could be lurking—

She squinted. Was that someone crouching behind that Ford truck? She thought she could make out the top of a head above the bed of the truck. Was someone waiting there, watching her? Her heartbeat quickened as the hair lifted on the back of her neck.

"Who's there?"

Footsteps.

Scuffling closer.

It had not been the wind stirring the soda can.

Andie peered into the darkness but couldn't see past the first row of cars. Dim light and shadows made it difficult to tell the color of nearby cars—or what lay beyond them.

"I know you're there!"

A man suddenly stood and stepped from behind the truck. He didn't move; just watched. He was dressed all in black: sweatpants, sweatshirt, a sports cap on his head. A bright sports logo was on the bill of his dark cap. Too dark to see clearly. Only his face was really visible.

He held something behind his back. Was it a gun? A knife?

Andie spun around, looked up at the elevator's panel. The red light indicated it was on the top floor—probably delivering Tanner to the suite.

No time to wait.

She ran in the opposite direction, passing rows of cars, slipping between them. She didn't know where she was going. She didn't know if this would lead her out of the building. Maybe it would lead her further into the parking garage.

He followed her, athletic shoes squawking against blacktop. "Hey, come back here!"

Her breath caught in her throat. Mouth dry.

Can't breathe.

What did he want? Who was it? Was it Brian? Had he returned for her? She hadn't seen him in over ten years. Would she be able to recognize him?

His footsteps became louder, his breath more labored as he drew closer.

And then he grabbed her. He pulled the hem of her shirt and yanked, causing her to stumble. She lost her balance and cried out as she collapsed. She looked up, saw him above, and rolled under a nearby truck. He bent at the waist and grabbed her foot, pulling her out.

"No!" she cried, kicking out at him with her other foot. "Let me go!"

Andie's foot connected with his hand. He released her and she used those precious seconds to scramble back under and scoot to the other side. Clambering out, she stood to find him coming around the other side of the truck.

Fast, how could he be so fast?

"Hey, I just wanna talk to you!"

A white shuttle bus suddenly turned the corner, bathing them in golden light. She ran toward the shuttle and caught the driver's startled reaction as he slammed on the brakes.

Bursts of light. The whirl of a camera. She looked over her shoulder to see the man snapping pictures of her. He lowered the camera and yanked a small wire bound notepad out of his pocket.

"Ms. Thornburg, can you tell me where you've been these past ten years? Can you tell me who kidnapped you so long ago? Can you—"

A reporter. *Just a damn reporter.*
Andie clenched her fists, fury replacing fear. "You creep! How dare you chase me!"
The shuttle driver stuck his head out. "Ma'am, you okay?"
"Mrs. Thornburg—"The reporter stepped forward but was violently pushed. His ball cap flew off as he landed on his hands and knees.
Andie looked up. Jared stood over the reporter. Tanner stood beside him.
"Andie, what's going on?" Tanner asked. "Are you okay?" He turned and looked at the reporter. "And just who the hell are you?"
The reporter climbed to his feet, reached for his ball cap and adjusted it on his head. He withdrew a badge with his name and picture on it. "Elliott Newman, *New York Times.*"
Elliott Newman swore at Jared as the bodyguard yanked his arm behind his back and forced him to his knees. "Hey, hold on. You can't treat me this way!"
Tanner stepped forward. "Were you harassing my wife?"
"No, sir. Just trying to get some information, sir."
The shuttle driver stepped out and Tanner turned his anger and confusion on the young boy. "What the hell is going on?"
The kid held up one hand; the other clenched a clipboard. He looked too young to drive. "I'm here to pick up a Mrs. Thornburg."
"Jared, take care of Newman," Tanner said.
As Jared pushed them away, Tanner glared at Andie. "You know anything about this?"
"Yes."
"And where were you going to go?"
"Home."
"And where is that, exactly?" Tanner said. He then glanced at the boy. "You can leave." He reached for his wallet and pulled out a ten dollar bill, handing it to the driver. "For your trouble."
"Thanks." The driver climbed inside and drove away,

disappearing up the ramp.

"I want to go home!"

"I thought you wanted to stay. You were more than happy to go with me back at the police station!"

"I've changed my mind."

"How can you call that place home? You lived on the streets. Lived out of garbage cans!"

"What do you think I am? An animal? I never lived out of garbage cans! I always found ways to get the money I needed to buy food!"

"By stealing?"

"Whatever it took!"

"By prostituting yourself?"

Andie lifted her hand to slap him but then lowered it, letting it sag to her side. Let the ignorant bastard believe what he wants, she thought. If he believed that, he wasn't worth it.

Tanner had expected her to deny it. When she didn't, he wouldn't even look at her. He believed his own words.

"I'm sorry, Andie," he mumbled.

She refused to look at him as she whispered, "Yes, so am I."

~ Twelve ~

She slept. Gone was the fierce scowl she had worn since leaving Detroit. For once, peace relaxed her features.

She'd argued all the way to the airport after Tanner announced they would immediately leave for New York City. He heard it all. How unhappy she was. How could he just take her against her will?

But was she really not happy? Did she really want to return to her life before? It was too late for that, he thought. She would be recognized wherever she went. The reporter in the parking garage proved that.

On the plane, Tanner watched Andie sleep from where he sat across the aisle. Her head rested uncomfortably against a window. Earlier, when he tried to offer her a pillow, her look of contempt silenced him.

Tanner glanced at his watch. It was time to wake her up and have her prepare for their arrival in New York. She would hate him even more when she heard what he had to say. She would need to get ready, change clothes before stepping off the plane. They couldn't be seen wearing T-shirts and jeans.

Tanner crossed the aisle. He lifted a hand and lightly touched the top of her head, brushing away curls that had escaped her ponytail.

"Andie, wake up. We're almost there."

She awoke slowly, languidly, stretching like a cat in the sun, before she realized who had awoken her and how close he was. And then the mask of rage settled once more on her beautiful features and she regarded him through narrowed eyes. "What do you want?"

"We're almost there. You should get ready."

"I *am* ready."

"You can't possibly wear—"

"What's wrong with this?"

"You can't wear jeans and a T-shirt to greet the press," Tanner said, rubbing his face. "And what will Ron say?"

"Ron?"

"You don't remember Ron? You hired him to be my advisor over ten years ago."

"I don't remember." Her gaze traveled down his clothing. "Is that what you're wearing?"

"I'm changing into a suit."

"You do that, and I'll wait up here for you."

Tanner lowered his face to hers; so close she could smell the wine he'd drunk earlier. "I'm not asking you, Andie."

She fingered her T-shirt as a thought came to her. Tanner wanted her to change for his appearance. She would obey, but that didn't mean she had to like it.

~~~~

What was taking her so long?

Tugging at his silk tie, Tanner stopped his frantic pacing to glance at his gold watch. The plane had landed five minutes ago and Andie was still locked in the lavatory.

Tanner rapped on the bathroom door. "Andie, are you almost finished? What's taking so long?"

"I'm almost done. It'll be worth the wait!"

Jared appeared at Tanner's side. "Sir, it's time. I'll get Andie. We have to move now. The crowd is getting impatient." Jared steered Tanner toward the back of the private plane, where a set of stairs was being positioned outside the door.

Tanner glanced out a small window and saw a large crowd outside. Reporters strained at the barricades. Citizens waved miniature New York state flags. His senior advisor, Ron Schultz, stood in front of the crowd, as stoic as the police officers around him.

Tanner's stomach pitched. What would Ron think of Andie?

It was no secret within his staff that Tanner despised Ron. After his appointment to governor, Ron had changed. He began to rule both the state and Tanner with an iron fist.

Tanner was afraid Ron would try to do the same with Andie. That's because Ron only thought about one thing: re-election. He would have fired him long ago but Ron was the best at what he did. Tanner would never have been elected if it wasn't for Ron. He was a true politician, ambitious and willing to do anything to get his way.

Tanner caught movement from the corner of his eye. He smelled Andie's perfume before he actually saw her. As he turned to greet her, Jared stepped in his way and began guiding him down the stairs.

Behind him, he heard Andie's startled cry when she saw the crowds behind the police barricades. He wanted to grab her hand but Jared was in the way.

The door opened, buffeting Tanner's hair as he hurried down the stairs. He lifted a hand and waved to the sea of faces, a wide smile spreading across his face. A cacophony of cameras clicked like Morse code as photographers battled each for the best shot.

He looked over his shoulder and saw a glimpse of Andie's hair.

One reporter pushed another out of the way and almost hit Tanner in the face as he shouted, "Sir, can you tell me your reaction when you found your wife?"

"Governor, what are your plans now that you found your wife after all these years?"

Ron Schultz stepped away from a limousine parked behind him and hurried toward Tanner, black coat flapping in the wind. His graying hair lifted from the fingers of the wind; he patted it carefully in place before stopping in front of Tanner.

"Governor, good to have you home again." He offered his free hand. His other held a bouquet of roses. "I brought Andra flowers. I remember she used to love roses."

Tanner accepted the handshake. "It's good to be home, Ron."

Ron's coat whipped again in the wind, revealing a black three-piece suit. Even at the airport, he dressed to impress.

With his cold blue hooded eyes and down turned mouth, Ron Schultz had once been described as 'the governor's intimidation force,' in the *New York Times*.

"Who needs security when Governor Thornburg has Ron Schultz beside him?" the reporter had quipped.

His senior advisor's constant frowns and thoughtful expressions had permanently worn furrows in his forehead, made more apparent by his rapidly receding hairline. Tanner had seen him smile only once – after Tanner won the race for governor.

Ron looked over Tanner's shoulder. "Where's that beautiful wife of yours? My God, can you believe this is really happening? I mean, after all this time she's back!"

Tanner reached behind him. Felt her small hand slip inside his. He pulled her away from Jared and said, "Ron, look who we finally found after all these years."

Ron smiled and stepped forward. "Andra, it's good to—" When Andie stepped out from behind Tanner, Ron lowered the bouquet. His smile fell into his customary frown.

Tanner turned to see what had put that expression on his face and stopped breathing when he saw his wife.

Heavy mascara. Black, smudged eyeliner. Caked foundation. Garish red lipstick.

"Andie?"

She looked like a streetwalker.

"*Andie?*" Tanner looked back at Ron. "Uh, I don't know what to say, Ron. She's not usually—"

"This—this isn't Andra!" Ron narrowed his eyes. "It—it can't be!"

"Oh, I am," Andie said, leaning against Tanner. "Hard to believe, isn't it?"

Tanner's eyes swept down her body. He should have been ashamed when he noticed what she was wearing. He should have been enraged. What he should *not* have been was aroused.

A black silk blouse was unbuttoned almost to her navel, exposing a black, lacy bra and creamy breasts straining over silky cups. A thick knot, tied above her belly button, was the only thing keeping it together. Stonewashed jeans hung so low they revealed hip bones. If they were a little bit lower they would reveal much more.

Tanner bowed his head and cleared his throat.

"Sir...sir, are you sure?" Ron straightened, suddenly aware of the cameras ticking in the background. The reporters were silent, the first time he had ever witnessed that happen. He knew it wouldn't be long until they found their voice again.

Wrestling out of his long coat, Ron stepped forward to wrap it around Andie but the look she gave was enough to stop him. He clutched his coat against his thighs and leaned closer to whisper, "Tanner, it looks like we're going to have to talk to her about appropriate attire. And what will the public think? The press will have a heyday with this. We need to get her out of here!"

Tanner grabbed Andie's elbow, steering her toward the limousine. He brushed his lips against her ear. "What is *wrong with you?*" He pushed her into the car's interior and followed her inside, his temper increasing as reporters shoved cameras and microphones at them.

Before Tanner could shut the door, Andie crawled on his lap and loosened his tie with steady, nimble fingers. "Now we can be alone, lover. Oh, I've waited so long for this!" Her hands slipped down his chest and brushed his groin.

"Andie!" Tanner clasped her wandering hands and moved his head away as she tried to nip his earlobe.

Andie trailed kisses over his face and lowered her mouth to his, dragging his lower lip between her teeth before slowly drawing away to whisper, "Come on, Tanner, don't be so shy." She lowered her mouth down his throat and flicked her tongue over his Adam's apple. "You weren't shy last night."

"Dammit, Andie, *will you stop!*" Tanner was too busy trying to capture Andie's roaming hands to shut the door. Cameras flashed, illuminating the interior. Capturing the scene that would be on the front of every New York newspaper.

Andie wriggled her fanny against his groin. "Tanner, make love to me!"

Tanner slammed the door shut and shouted for the driver to go. The limo lurched forward and pulled out of the airport.

With a triumphant smirk on her face, Andie drew away.

Tanner punched a button to raise the tinted privacy glass behind the driver's seat. In the dimness, Andie saw rage burning in his eyes as he said through clenched teeth, "Did you enjoy yourself, Andra?"

~ Thirteen ~

"Immensely!"

Tanner lashed out and wrapped his hand around her pale throat.

"Tanner, it was just a joke!" Andie clawed at his fingers as they tightened.

He had every right to choke her, she thought. She had acted like the streetwalker he presumed her to be. She'd embarrassed him.

But her plan of revenge aroused something other than his temper, she discovered as he pressed his groin against her crotch. "Well, this isn't a joke." His fingers softened as they stroked the smooth column of her throat.

As he ground his pelvis against hers, Andie attempted to scoot off him but he caught her waist and pushed her on the seat, pinning her against the leather seat.

"Tanner, it was a joke!"

Tanner caught her wrists and held them over her head. "And when you begged me to make love to you? To make you writhe against me? Was that a joke?"

"Yes!"

"Liar!"

"Get off me!"

"That's not what you were saying a minute ago."

"I don't want—"

Tanner silenced her protest with his mouth. His lips molded to hers, silently condemning her actions. And when she cried out, he lightened his kiss until he was silently beseeching, begging for forgiveness. His tongue claimed hers, meeting, withdrawing, meeting and withdrawing again until they were both breathless. He pulled away and turned his face into her hand, nipping lightly at her palm.

She tilted his face up and gazed down at him. He was beautiful. Long, inky black eyelashes created tiny fans when he closed his eyes. Full, sensuous lips. She wanted to tell him he was beautiful, but hesitated. Did a woman say such a thing to a man?

Andie shyly lowered her lips to his. She told herself to go

slow, but his deep, throaty groans spurred her like gasoline on fire. She came alive in his hands, reacting like never before. She grasped his face and melded her mouth over his, drawing away to test each angle, claiming first his upper lip, then his lower. She had denied her femininity by disguising it under bulky masculine clothing. Hid it from men and herself. She would be safer, she'd tried convincing herself. But dressed as she was now, she felt every inch the female she was.

She brushed her lips against his, once, twice, hesitantly at first and then harder and more selfishly. He wrapped his arms around her and sat forward to take over.

Andie pushed him against the leather seats. "It's my turn."

Tanner grinned lazily. "If you insist."

She ran her hands over his wide shoulders and then lowered them to untie his silk tie. As she fumbled impatiently with the knot, Tanner reached up and undid it for her and pulled it away. Her fingers quickly unbuttoned his shirt, and she pushed it away and let her eager gaze drift down his chest.

As Andie hesitantly touched his nipple, brushing her thumb over it, Tanner lowered his head on the back of the seat and groaned at her touch.

She expected shame. She expected embarrassment. But what she felt instead was overwhelming power that she could affect Tanner this much. Her touch alone made him groan and whisper her name. And if her touch made him react that way, what would her mouth do?

She lowered her mouth over his nipple.

Tanner stiffened and sat up so quickly Andie slipped off his lap and barely caught herself before tumbling to the floor of the limousine.

"Tanner? What is it?"

Tanner drew away, leaning against the window as he tried to steady his breathing.

"Tanner?"

He glared at her. "Do you move this fast with other men?"

"What?"

Tanner's jaw tightened. "Is this how you toy with the other men? Or am I getting special treatment?"

"You—you think I was a prostitute?"

"You were moving like there was no tomorrow. I'm not a fool!"

"Then don't act like one!"

Tanner looked out the window before she saw how crushed he was. The thought of Andie with another man made him want to put his fist through the tinted privacy window. He closed his eyes but remembered her cries and moans. Had it been staged? Did she moan like that for other men? Did her body respond to other men like it responded with him?

Tanner lowered the window as nausea settled in his stomach when he thought of Andie sharing her bed. Of what she had done with those men.

Andie's voice broke through his melancholy when she whispered, "Are you going to pay me for my services?"

Tanner's head snapped up. "Is that what you want?" He sneered. "But then that's what you've always wanted, isn't it, Andie? In the end, it's always about money!" Reaching into his back pocket, he withdrew his leather wallet and grabbed everything inside. Twenties, fifties, hundred dollar bills rained onto her lap.

"There, that's for services rendered!"

As money fluttered onto her lap, Andie looked out the window before Tanner saw tears brimming in her eyes. Her clever plan to humiliate him had backfired. In the end, she had been the one humiliated.

~ Fourteen ~

"We're here," Tanner mumbled, breaking nearly thirty minutes of silence.

Andie scooted to the edge of her seat as the limo slowed to a stop in front of high-rise apartments. Pressing her nose against the glass, she tilted her head back to see the top of the building but it was too high. She started to count the number of floors and stopped after sixteen.

The building had to be over twenty stories high.

Dozens of windows, bordered with strings of Christmas lights, flickered in a kaleidoscope of color. Christmas trees filled other windows, stars or angels winking from the tops.

"You live here?"

"I live in the Governor's Mansion in Albany but I've taken some time off."

"For me?"

"For us."

"Is this where we lived ten years ago?"

"Yes. Do you remember it?"

"No. Should I?"

"It was your parents' home. You grew up here."

"I don't remember."

"They gave it to us when they retired to Florida all those years ago."

She could see why he had never left. With garland adorning the street poles and snow layering the sidewalks, the city was beautiful and impressive. The large, intimidating buildings reminded her of downtown Detroit's business section, some so large they took up an entire city block. Crowds of people created an impenetrable wall as they bustled by the limousine. Most of them ignored it, as if accustomed to seeing limousines parked in front of the building.

"Which apartment's yours?"

"The top."

"The penthouse. Of course."

"One of my assistants will take care of you." Tanner climbed out and bent over, looking at her from outside. "Don't even think of going anywhere without an escort."

"I'm not a prisoner, or a child, so don't treat me like one!"

Tanner's eyes swept over her attire. "I have no doubt about that." Before she could say anything, he hurried up the marble steps. He nodded to a woman emerging from the lobby before he disappeared into the arched doorway.

The driver met her eyes in the rearview mirror. "I'll have your luggage sent up to your room, Mrs. Thornburg."

"Don't bother. Take me back to the airport, please."

He ignored her as he climbed out and walked to the back of the limo, popping open the trunk. It whined as he lifted the trunk lid. She heard him greet someone as he set her luggage on the curb.

"Evenin', Ms. Van Dyke."

"Evening, Mr. Allister. How are you doing?" a soft female voice replied.

"Couldn't be better, couldn't be better."

Andie twisted around to see who he was talking to but the trunk was still raised, blocking her view. She started to scoot toward the open door but a woman's face appeared.

"Welcome home, Mrs. Thornburg."

Andie lifted her head and hesitantly accepted the woman's hand as she climbed out and straightened. She became aware of how tall she was next to the petite woman. "Thanks."

"I'm Elizabeth Van Dyke, Governor Thornburg's assistant. I'll be helping you get settled in."

"It's nice to meet you."

"I've heard a lot about you, Mrs. Thornburg."

Andie forced a smile that didn't reach her eyes. What did that mean? Was it good or bad?

With her blond hair and blue eyes, Elizabeth Van Dyke looked to be about her age but her stylish brown suit made her appear older. Andie longed for female companionship. She missed the women she had talked and laughed with in the shelters. She didn't consider them friends; perhaps companions. She was careful to keep people at a distance because life on the street was hard; food, shelter and donations dictating where you went and when. And how long you stayed. Friendships were hard to maintain.

Andie reached for her luggage at the curb—one suitcase filled with all of her belongings. Another of Jared's purchases while staying in Detroit.

Elizabeth wrapped her fingers around Andie's elbow. "Leave it. Someone will bring it up soon."

"But it's no problem."

Elizabeth looked up and suddenly tensed. Andie turned to see why.

Several news vans pulled up behind the limousine, passenger doors opening before coming to a complete stop. Reporters jumped out and hurried toward Andie.

"Come on. We have to hurry." Elizabeth guided Andie up the steps and looked up as a doorman stepped out, holding the door for them.

"Ladies."

"Eric," Elizabeth said, brushing by him.

Behind them, a reporter shouted, "Mrs. Thornburg, can we have a minute?"

As Andie stepped inside the apartment building, the door closed behind her. She looked over her shoulder and saw the doorman struggling to push reporters away.

"Mrs. Thornburg, we should get you upstairs."

Speechless, Andie gazed at the lobby. A large fountain six tiers high bubbled from the center of the room. Water, so blue it had to be dyed, raced off each level before falling to the bottom. Copper pennies shimmered from below the surface.

"Wow!"

"That was my first reaction too." Elizabeth pointed up. "But wait until you see this."

Andie's jaw dropped as she tilted her head back.

"Well? What do you think?"

"I think…I think it's beautiful."

The interior of the building was shaped in a circle, the middle left open for shock factor, the fountain being the focal point. As Andie watched, two kids on the second floor leaned against the glass partition and dropped pennies into the fountain below. The center of each floor became more shadowed the higher Andie looked. The building's floors were apparent only from the strings of white Christmas lights wrapped around the partitions. They shimmered like stars from above.

"It—it almost makes you dizzy looking up," Andie said.

"Wait until you're up there looking down."

"I bet it's beautiful."

Glass elevators were positioned in each corner, delivering occupants to their floors. A family of four stepped off on the fourth floor. A single man carrying a briefcase was entering another one on the first floor.

Elizabeth pointed to an empty conference room. "When there are a lot of us, the governor sometimes holds meetings there."

Track lighting reflected off the green marbled floors. As they walked toward the elevators, Andie almost slipped on the polished surface and caught herself before she fell.

"Are you okay?" Elizabeth asked, stopping in front of the elevators.

"Yes, I'm fine," Andie said, watching her reflection waver in the glass doors as she waited for them to open. She realized then how ridiculous she looked dressed that way, her hair teased and heavy black eyeliner framing her eyes. She felt like a fool. What must Tanner think?

The doors opened and they stepped inside. As the elevator rose, Andie edged closer to the door and looked out as the water fountain shrank until she could no longer see it.

"It's beautiful," she whispered, placing her hands on the glass door.

The elevator stopped. The doors opened.

"We're here." Elizabeth stepped out and hurried toward the penthouse suite, the only one on the floor. She turned to see that Andie wasn't behind her.

"Mrs. Thornburg?"

"I'm right over here." Andie gripped the glass partition's railing and gazed at the lobby below but was too high to make it out.

"Are you afraid of heights?"

"No," Andie said. "I just wanted to see what it looked like below."

"I'll show you inside."

"Is this the only apartment up here?"

"Governor Thornburg has the whole floor to himself."

Elizabeth knocked briefly before entering. "Governor? Are you here?" She dropped her keys on a glass table at the door. A matching mirror caught her reflection as she walked down the hallway, heels clicking on the black tile. She peeked into each room as she passed and looked over her shoulder and waved, indicating that Andie should follow.

"Governor Thornburg?"

Elizabeth turned left and entered the living room. Green suede furniture was formed into the shape of an L and faced a big screen television. A matching suede armchair and ottoman flanked the television. The television was off. The only sound came from a fireplace crackling in the center of the room.

Andie reached out and fingered the suede couch. "Where is he?"

Elizabeth walked across the room and stopped in front of a closed door. She lowered her voice and said, "This is the Governor's office while he's in town. He's apparently in here. We'll leave him alone for now."

He was probably still upset with her, Andie thought as Elizabeth gave her a tour. She was shown the library, kitchen, family room, exercise room and finally Andie's bedroom.

Elizabeth turned on the light and entered a room done entirely in red and black. A vase of yellow roses sat on each bed stand, flanking the large canopied bed.

"This is where I'll stay?"

"This was your room." Elizabeth crossed the bedroom and turned on the brass lamp beside the bed. "Before your disappearance."

"I stayed here?"

"Yes."

"Where's Tanner's room?"

"Across the hall."

"We...didn't stay in the same room?"

Elizabeth looked away as she fluffed the sham pillows. "Uh, I don't know anything about that."

"I understand things were … strained."

"I don't know. It was before my time." Elizabeth nodded at the closet. "Your clothes are inside. Everything is as you left it."

"Everything was saved?"

"Yes."

Soft ceiling lights bathed the room, spilling across a red leather sofa and matching recliner in the corner of the room. A plush black rug covered the wooden floors, looking suspiciously like animal fur. Two separate rooms branched off the bedroom.

"The bathroom and walk-in closet," Elizabeth said.

Andie entered the bathroom and flipped the light. The bathroom was divided into two rooms, with linen closets separating them. A large tub big enough to fit two people filled the first room. The white tiled floor contrasted sharply against the black towels suspended on a towel bar.

"That tub is enormous!"

"It's a Jacuzzi."

At Andie's blank stare, Elizabeth pointed to the buttons located outside the tub. "A whirlpool, you know?"

Andie nodded like she understood but had no idea what she was talking about. She walked past the linen closets and entered the other room. A shower stood in one corner. Andie opened the glass door and looked inside. The shower's interior was also done entirely in white tile. On the shower's floor lay a pattern of brightly colored tile—red, orange, violet and blue. When she looked more closely, she made out the image of a butterfly.

Elizabeth folded her arms and leaned against the door-frame. "It's called a mosaic."

"It's beautiful." Andie slipped her fingers through metal holes in the walls of the shower stall. There were four, spaced about three inches apart. They ran the length of the shower and stopped about two feet off the ground. "What are these?"

"Jets."

"Jets?"

"Jets of water you can turn on while you're showering."

"Why?"

Elizabeth lifted a shoulder. "I don't know."

Andie shut the glass shower door with a click. "Weird."

Elizabeth looked at her watch. "I hate to run but Ron and I are supposed to meet the Governor in a few minutes to catch up on news."

Andie opened and shut the console's drawers and saw toothpaste, toothbrushes, make-up and mouthwash. Everything was new. "No, you go ahead. I can handle it from here."

"When they arrive with your luggage, I'll tell them to set it outside your room."

"Okay."

"It was nice finally meeting you." Elizabeth backed out of the room, leaving Andie alone.

Andie shut off the bathroom light and stopped in front of the walk-in closet. She opened it and fumbled for the light switch. When it came on, she saw shawls, sweaters, fur coats, gowns. Probably over thirty pairs of high heels. Had these all been hers?

Reaching up, she fingered the sleeve of a fur coat. She looked at the tag. Mink. *Real mink?*

She couldn't wear any of these. They just weren't practical. As she shut the closet door and sank on the bed, she slipped off her shoes and socks, lowering her feet to the fur rug. She curled her toes in it, delighting in the feel of it against her feet.

Suddenly an idea hit her. She could—

Andie lifted her head as the door suddenly opened. "Elizabeth, I don't need…"

But it wasn't Elizabeth's slender body that filled the bedroom door. It was Ron Schultz. His eyes narrowed as he watched her from the doorway with arms crossed over his chest.

Andie sat up. "What do you want?" She saw something missing in his eyes. Maybe it was because he didn't look at people. He looked through them or past them, but never *at* them.

Ron leaned against the doorframe. "I see you've made yourself comfortable."

"Is there something you want?"

"I want the truth." Ron shut the door and crossed to the bed, glaring down at her. "Who are you? Why are you here?"

"Just what are you trying to pull?"

"Perhaps I should ask the same of you, Andra. If that's even your real name."

"You don't believe I'm her?"

"Of course you aren't her. You may have fooled Tanner, but you can't fool me. The Andra Thornburg I remember would never dress slutty." Ron lowered his voice as he added, "What do you want? Money?"

"I want to go home."

She regretted agreeing to go with Tanner at the police station. Her intentions—as deceitful as they were—were to get some food, get a few nights good rest, maybe take some money when he wasn't looking and then leave him for good.

But the most unexpected thing had happened. She had started to fall for Tanner. She couldn't stay now.

"That's it? Nothing else? Then why put on this farce?"

"I didn't ask for this."

"I do believe Tanner was thinking with another part of his body when he brought you here. Unless you really *are* Andra."

"Get out of my room."

"I want proof that you're Andra." Ron lowered his eyes to her bare ankle. "I want to see the birthmark. You don't mind if I look, do you?"

Before she could respond, he knelt and grabbed her ankle, exposing the birthmark. He furiously rubbed it, but it didn't disappear. Dropping her ankle, he whispered, "My God, it's

her. It—it's *you.*" He straightened and backed away.
Several moments passed while he composed himself.
"Tanner's up for re-election next year. If you mess that up for
him, I'll make you regret it!"
Andie watched as Ron left as quickly as he had come.

~ Fifteen ~

He hadn't talked to his wife in two days. And the few
times she had seen him in passing, she refused to acknowledge
him. Was she still mad about the incident in the limousine?
Was she that unhappy with him? She had everything she could
ever want—wealth, servants, the penthouse. What more could
she want?

Tanner trudged to his bedroom, tugging off his tie. He
had been in meetings for the last two days, something that had
kept him away from his wife. Was that why she was mad? Did
she feel that he had deserted her?

The telephone interviews with several newspapers and
television shows had all asked for one thing: an interview with
Andie. He refused. It was too soon to subject her to that. He
answered their questions but they continued to call him.

Tanner entered his bedroom and shut the door behind
him. He threw his tie on the bed and began unbuttoning his
dress shirt. Crossing to the walk-in closet, he threw open the
door and turned on the light.

And stared inside.

It was empty. The only occupants were hangers and dust
bunnies clinging to the corners.

"What the…"

Tanner closed the door. Had they had a burglary?

He crossed to the Monet hanging on the wall—*The
Artist's Garden at Giverny*—and lifted the painting from the
wall. His safe was hidden behind it, set into the wall. Twisting
the tarnished brass dial, he heard the tumblers engage. He
opened the door and saw his money inside.

"What the hell is going on?" He reached for the phone and dialed Jared's cell. How could anybody get inside? He had guards patrolling the lobby downstairs. What else had been taken? And why only his clothes? Why—

"Hello?"

"Jared, it's me."

"Something wrong, Governor?" He thought better of telling Jared.

"No, I'm sorry for bothering you." He set the phone down carefully in the cradle, trying to contain his emotions as they fired one after the other—confusion, fear, finally anger.

Andie.

Tanner grabbed the doorknob, twisted and yanked his door open. It banged against the wall as he entered the hallway and crossed the short span to her room. Throwing open her door, he saw her lying belly-first on the bed, a magazine spread open in front of her. Her legs were crossed, her feet bare.

It smelled like nail polish inside.

She jerked her head up and glared at him. "Mind knocking next time?"

Tanner slammed the door behind him. "What have you done?"

Andie rolled onto her back and drew to her elbows, watching him warily.

"Where are they?"

"If you're talking about your clothes, they're in the same place mine are." She nodded toward her walk-in closet.

Tanner dropped his hands on his hips. "Which is…?"

"By now? Probably on their way to several homeless shelters around town."

"What?"

"I donated them."

"*You did what?* I can't believe you donated my clothes to homeless shelters!"

"They need it more than you do!"

"Is this to get back at me for what happened in the limo?"

"No!"

"Is it because you've been left on your own these past few days?"

Andie drew to her feet. "It's because it was the right thing to do! If you'd only open your eyes and get your head out of your—"

"If you want to donate your clothes, that's fine, but leave mine alone!" Tanner swore under his breath and began pacing the room. "My shoes. My suits. My ties. Everything...gone?"

"I cleaned out the cupboards too, and donated the food."

"The *food?*"

"You're so selfish, Tanner. You don't realize how good you've got it!"

"And you don't realize how much that stuff was worth! What the hell am I going to wear now? I am the *governor* of New York. I can't possibly wear—"

"My point exactly!"

"What the hell are you talking about?"

"Open your eyes and see what's around you for once! Do your job. People are starving and freezing on the streets out there and you're complaining because you—"

"Funding—"

"That's just an excuse, Governor."

"So now it's Governor, is it?"

Andie tried to brush by him but he grabbed her elbow. "You shouldn't have done that, Andie. It wasn't right."

"No," she said. "That's where you have it wrong. I *did* do the right thing. And that's what you won't ever understand unless you open your eyes, Tanner. Unless you go out there, on the streets and see what people refuse to see."

He lowered his hand. She swept by him and out the door.

~ Sixteen ~

"This is big, Governor," Elizabeth Van Dyke said. "This is what we've been waiting for to boost your ratings!"

"I disagree," replied Ron. "I think it might hurt your ratings if you reveal too much."

Tanner's leather chair creaked as he leaned back. "I don't want Andie involved."

The three of them were gathered in Tanner's office. Elizabeth set her coffee mug down on the corner of the governor's desk. "Not involve Andra? Governor, this whole thing involves her. The press is demanding to see her. Your supporters want to see her. Use this opportunity to boost your ratings!" She stood and walked to the window. Lifting a hand, she pointed toward the street. "People are lined up outside to see her, to speak with her. People are fascinated by her sudden re-appearance. They want to know what happened."

"This is ridiculous." Tanner lifted his coffee mug to his lips. "I will not exploit her."

Ron steepled his fingers and peered suspiciously at his boss. "Just what did happen, Governor? Where has she been all these years?"

Tanner hesitated. He didn't want them to know Andie's background. Was it because he wanted to protect her? Or because he was embarrassed? And how could he keep this to himself? Elizabeth was right. It couldn't be kept secret for long. Not in his position.

"Just one interview." Elizabeth leaned a hip against the wall. "All the networks are clamoring for an interview. You have your choice."

"No."

"Just think what it could do for your ratings. Think about the future. Think about how far you've come these ten years," she said. "You weren't even mayor when she disappeared and now you're governor of New York! We used your wife's disappearance to tug on voter's heartstrings and it worked. It could happen again. It—"

"It was wrong!" Tanner said. "I don't want to exploit this. Not now. Not again."

"Re-election is coming up," Elizabeth said. "This story

would guarantee another four years."

"I disagree," Ron said. "It might hurt his chances."

"I am not going to exploit my wife! Why can't you understand that?"

Ron lifted his head. "She would never have hesitated to exploit *you*, Governor."

Tanner narrowed his eyes. "You go too far, Ron. She's changed. She's not the person she once was."

Elizabeth lifted her hands in surrender. "Okay, okay. We're just watching out for you, doing our jobs."

"I appreciate it, I do," Tanner said, meaning it. He would never be where he was if it weren't for these two people in front of him. "But my wife has been through hell and back. I won't put her through it again."

"So tell me. Is she…you know…" Ron said, tapping his head.

"What?" Tanner said.

"Is she all right, you know, in the head?"

"Of course she is!"

Ron shrugged. "Well, you never know. Ten years is a long time. A lot can happen to someone in that time."

"What are you getting at?"

Ron met Tanner's eyes. "Nothing, sir."

~~~~~

Someone knocked.

Andie lifted her head from the book she was reading. "Who is it?"

Elizabeth Van Dyke opened the bedroom door. "It's me."

Andie tried not to look too disappointed when it wasn't Tanner. She hadn't seen him all day and she found herself missing him. Was he still upset with her? Had she spoiled his chances at re-election, like Ron feared?

She didn't want to be responsible for ruining his career. It meant too much to him. She felt terrible about the stunt at the airport.

"How—how are you?" Elizabeth said, struggling for small talk. "Are you all settled in?"

"I believe so."

"How are you coping?"

"Okay, I guess."

"Do you remember any of this?"

"Not much."

"What do you remember? What happened to you?"

Andie guessed that Elizabeth wasn't too much older than herself. She would have been pretty if she didn't always look so stressed or wear clothing that made her appear fifteen years older. She frowned and said, "Tanner hasn't told you?"

"The governor is keeping it pretty top secret, whatever *it* is."

Andie tried not to look hurt. So he *was* embarrassed of her. Or maybe he hadn't had time to tell his staff members. She would have to talk to him about it.

"Mrs. Thornburg, I didn't mean to get sidetracked but would you come with me into the living room, please? There's somebody who wants to see you."

Andie sat up. "Who?"

"Ron Schultz—"

"What does he want?"

"If you could just come with me, ma'am."

"Let me get dressed and I'll be out in a minute."

Elizabeth nodded and shut the door.

What did Ron want with her? Andie sighed and crawled off the bed. Her jeans lay in a pile. They might be a little worn but they were comfortable. She put them on and grabbed her old flannel shirt. She slipped her winter coat on, walked out of her room and entered the living room.

Ron paced in front of the fireplace. Elizabeth looked out the window, her arms crossed over her chest. When he saw her, his face blanched. "Good God, you look a wreck!"

Andie frowned. "What do you want?"

"Elizabeth," Ron said, looking at Elizabeth, "we have our work cut out for us."

~~~~

The limousine stopped.

"Where's Tanner?" Andie pressed her face against the window and looked outside.

Ron climbed out of the limo and helped Elizabeth out. He then offered his hand to Andie. She remained where she was seated.

"Get out, Andra."

"Where's Tanner?"

Ron grabbed her wrist but she recoiled from his touch and climbed out on her own.

"He had some work to do," Ron said, closing the door.

"You told me we were meeting him for a late lunch!"

"So I lied." Ron pushed her ahead of him. "Now walk."

"Why are we here?" Andie looked over her shoulder at Elizabeth, who followed meekly behind Ron. "What do you want?"

"You'll find out when we get there now, won't you?" Ron came up beside her and grabbed her elbow, his fingers digging painfully into her flesh.

Andie grimaced but refused to cry out.

"The Governor asked that we take you out to do some things," Ron said.

"I already have clothes," she said. "Elizabeth bought some for me."

"Then why aren't you wearing them?"

"I don't like them."

"Then we'll get you something you like," he said. "You can't be seen in public like this."

Andie looked at Ron. Why had Tanner sent her with this man? She didn't like him or his orders but she would go along with them because they were her husband's wishes. She would do this to make up for embarrassing him at the airport.

They went around the street corner and stopped outside Rainey's Hair and Nail Salon. A homeless man sat in the doorway, his hat cockeyed over his forehead, shielding the sun from his face; a face that used the doorframe for a pillow. He appeared to be dozing.

"Christ," Ron said, throwing up his hands. "Can't they do something about this in this city? Can't a man go anywhere anymore without seeing this garbage polluting our—"

"Hey," Andie said. "It's not his fault—"

"It's never their fault," Ron replied and reached out to shake the man awake but then thought better of it. He lifted his foot.

"If you kick that man, I'll kick you!"

Ron looked over his shoulder and glared at Andie. He opened his mouth to reply but was distracted when the man suddenly awoke and jumped to his feet. He glanced shyly at Ron before sidling past him and racing off.

Andie pulled her arm out of Ron's tight grasp. "Why are we here?"

"To do what Tanner should have done days ago," Ron said and then looked back at Elizabeth. "They know we're coming?"

"Yes."

"They've been warned not to say anything to anybody?"

"They closed the business for the afternoon to comply with us," Elizabeth replied.

"What's going on?" Andie said.

Ron opened the salon's door. "You, my dear, are going to have a complete makeover."

~ Seventeen ~

The acetone used during the manicure was giving Andie a headache. A swiveling tower fan blew from behind the row of black sinks but it only seemed to make the harsh chemicals more noticeable. It permeated the room until Andie could no longer smell her coconut-scented hair, until she was forced to breathe through her mouth.

She bent her head and sipped at her strawberry-banana drink—something called a "smoothie"—that the manager had blended for her in the kitchenette, the latest rage in hair salons according to Elizabeth.

Andie watched in the mirror as a stylist swept clips of dark hair off the ceramic tile floor—Andie's hair. She wanted to reach up and touch her newly shorn hair—nearly four inches gone—but her nails were still wet.

She lifted her free hand and admired the muted brown-gold color she had picked ... almost the color of Tanner's eyes, she realized.

Blue, black and red brushes littered the small countertop in front of her, competing for space with the hair dryer, tangled curling irons and a tall glass filled with purple jelly-like liquid. Andie leaned out of the chair to study the jar. For sterilization purposes, she realized as she read the label. She sat back and took another sip of her smoothie.

Her foot tingled, reminding her that she had been in the same position for over 20 minutes—*when were they going to leave?* She uncrossed her legs and rested her barefoot once more on the cold metal rest of the stylist's chair. For the first time since she could remember, polish covered her toenails.

Out of the corner of her eye, she saw Ron watching her from where he sat in another styling chair beside the window, legs crossed, a *Time* magazine closed in his lap. She turned her head and gasped when she saw the cover: a picture of herself. The headline—

Found! NY Governor Greets Long-Lost Wife—topped the picture in large white type.

Ron placed the magazine on the counter. "What do you think of the new you?"

Andie shrugged. "It's okay."

"You don't like it?" Ron cocked his head and studied her. "I think they did a superb job. It's like that old story, the one about the ugly duckling and the swan."

Andie bristled from the insult but bit her tongue. For over three hours, she had endured a roomful of women fussing over her. She had suffered a manicure and pedicure, facial and waxed eyebrows.

Glancing at herself in the mirror, she caught her lower lip between her teeth. She didn't recognize the person staring back at her. Her hair was styled, teased in the front and sides, and had been sprayed with so much hairspray her head felt like a helmet.

She looked like the streetwalkers in Detroit. What would Tanner say? Is this what he wanted her to look like?

Ron folded his arms. "So tell me, where have you been, Andra?"

"What?"

"These past ten years," he said. "Why didn't you come forward until now?"

"I didn't," she said. "I…" *got arrested*, she almost said. "I suffered memory loss. I was living in Michigan."

"Doing what?"

Elizabeth entered the salon just then, saving her from answering. Tanner's young assistant walked up to them and sat beside Andie, slinging several garment bags over her lap. "Wow, I didn't even recognize you!"

"Uh, thanks." Had that been a compliment or an insult?

"I bought some clothes I thought you might like." Elizabeth pushed the garment bags at her. "Why don't you change out of those nasty clothes?"

"I want to go home."

"Not until you change."

"Then can we go home?"

"No, then we go to the medical clinic," Ron said, appearing behind her.

~~~~~

"I won't do it!"

"You're making a spectacle of yourself. Now do what they say!"

"I will not take my clothes off! Take me back."

Andie climbed off the examination table and started for the door but Ron grabbed her elbow. He yanked her closer until she could smell his peppermint-laced breath.

"You *will* undergo a physical exam, Andra. You *will* submit to having tests done. I—I won't have you ruin the Governor's reputation."

"Nobody is touching me!"

Their argument was gaining the attention of the doctors and nurses. Andie lifted her head and met the eyes of Dr. Bryce Overt, the physician who had alerted Ron that she was being obstinate, refusing to change into a hospital gown.

Ron pushed her back into the small room. Charts and diagrams of the human body lined the walls. Medical instruments, cotton balls, a syringe, tongue prongs, a vial of smelling salts. They all lined a metal tray that sat on the counter beside the sink.

"It's a risk being here," he said. "Do this and then we can go."

"Risk for whom? You?"

She knew that soon after leaving the salon, paparazzi had begun to follow them. Whose attention was he more worried about? The press? The public? Or Tanner's?

"We need to rule out diseases and—"

"I don't have a disease!"

"How do we know that?" Ron softly shut the door.

Andie glanced at the hospital gown that lay folded on the examination table. "Tanner doesn't know I'm here, does he?"

"You'll either do this—"

"They want to test me for STDs! Do you know how humiliating that is?"

Ron grabbed her shoulders. "Listen, lady. You've been gone for ten years. God knows what you did during that time.

You could have been shooting heroin, prostituting yourself and who knows what else. The Governor needs to know that you're healthy!"

"You mean *you* need to know!"

"Okay, I need to know," Ron said. "For Tanner's sake. He should have done it days ago. I just hope it's not too late."

"What do you mean?"

"Do I have to spell it out for you?" Ron shoved the hospital gown at her. "You are husband and wife. I only hope that he hasn't slept with you yet until we know—"

"That is none of your business!"

Andie clenched the hospital gown against her chest. She didn't mind the examination at first. They checked her blood pressure and temperature but when they said they would need to give her a gynecological exam and pregnancy test, followed by a blood test, she panicked.

She endured the makeover. But this…this was degrading. She couldn't go through with it. Not now, not with Ron making her do it.

As if reading her mind, Ron said, "Do it, or it'll ruin the Governor's reputation."

She put on her clothes. She couldn't do it. She wouldn't let him degrade her like that. Spinning around, she pushed past Ron and fled the room.

She didn't know where she was. She didn't know where to go. She just ran. Down one hallway and then another, past a startled nurse and receptionist. She saw the exit sign above a door ahead and ran for it.

She exited the building, breathing hard. Stopping, she looked left and right. Where was she? Where was the main street? If she could get there, she could—

She was stuck. She had no money to hail a cab.

"Andra, wait!" Ron cried out from behind.

She looked over her shoulder as he burst from the clinic. She turned and began running down the alley. The street was ahead, cars whizzing by, a bus stopped in front to let people off.

She ran out of the alley and stopped on the street corner. Which way should she go? She had no idea where she was.

"Mrs. Thornburg?" A woman pushing a stroller stopped suddenly in front of her. "Andra Thornburg, is that you? I just saw your picture in the paper. I'm sure glad—"

And then Ron was behind her.

"Andra, wait!" he said, grabbing her wrist.

"Leave me alone!"

Another woman walking a dog looked at her. "It's the Governor's wife! Mrs. Thornburg, can I have your autograph?"

And that gained the attention of others. Cars began slowing down as they passed. She looked up to see the passengers on the bus point at her as the bus drew away from the curb.

She had to escape.

Ron stepped forward as she shied away. "Andra, where do you think you're going?"

Cars suddenly appeared at the curb. Reporters climbed out, surrounding her. She tried to push her way through them but they waved microphones in front of her and she was blinded by strobe-like flashes from the cameras.

"Mrs. Thornburg, can you tell us where you've been these past ten years?"

"Mrs. Thornburg, what was your husband's reaction when you were found?"

"Ma'am, can you tell us how you felt when you saw your husband again?"

Andie pushed her away through the crowd. "Get out of my way! Leave me alone!"

The swelling crowd jostled her. Soon, she could find no way out of the mass of people. She sank to her knees while they fired question after question at her.

"Ma'am, can you tell me why you were at the clinic?"

"Mrs. Thornburg, can you tell us what happened so long ago? Did somebody take you, Andra?"

Shrieking brakes silenced the crowd. Reporters parted as if by a silent command. Andie looked up to see Tanner in front of her. He bent down and without a word, picked her up in her arms, cradling her against his chest. Turning, he let his security hold back the reporters as he hurried toward the limousine he had arrived in.

"Governor, do you have a minute to tell us how you felt upon your wife's sudden reappearance?"

"Governor Thornburg, what was your reaction when you heard she had been found?"

"No comment." He stopped briefly in front of the limousine to set her softly inside. He grabbed the blanket one of his guards tossed his way and wrapped her in it before settling down beside her and closing the door.

Tanner turned toward her but didn't say anything as he gathered her in his arms, stroking her hair and rocking her.

Andie closed her eyes and clung to his shirt. "Take me home, Tanny, please."

She didn't know who was more stunned at the use of his nickname—him or her. They slowly drew away from each other.

"You remember," he whispered.

She met his eyes. She had remembered. But what else lay in the deep well of her memories? She closed her eyes and tried to let others surface but they rested just out of her mental grasp.

Tanner cupped her face and tilted it back, pushing her hair away from her face. "What were you doing downtown? And what were you doing at the clinic? When the press called my office, wanting to know why you were there and if you had been hurt, I nearly went into shock."

Andie kept her face expressionless as her mind raced. Had he been concerned about her? Could he…care for her? She cleared her throat and said, "That's how you found me?"

"Yes."

"I—I came downtown to have my hair and make-up done." He couldn't know about Ron. Tanner would be enraged. Would he fire Ron? If so, it might hurt Tanner's chances of re-election.

"I can see that." Tanner touched her hair. "But that doesn't answer my question. Why were you at the clinic?" Tanner looked up as Ron pushed his way through the reporters, making his way toward the limousine. "And why was Ron with you? Were you hurt?"

"I...got something in my eyes at the salon. They had to flush them at the clinic."

"And Ron?"

"Ron escorted me downtown because I refused to have security with me. Said he—he would watch out for me." The words were difficult to say but she managed to force them up her constricted throat.

His fingers curled around her jaw as he turned her face toward him. "Your eyes look fine to me. And you even had time to apply your make-up again?" Tanner frowned. "I can't even see your face under all that make-up."

She was saved by Ron's voice outside the door, yelling to be let in. Tanner leaned over her and cracked the door open. Ron tumbled inside and sank against the seat across from them. He leaned his head against the headrest and closed his eyes. "They're crazy, all of 'em! Let's get out of here."

Tanner motioned to the driver to take off and they pulled away from the curb. Reporters continued to run beside the limousine until it picked up speed and left them behind.

Wrapping his arm around Andie's neck, he pulled her against him and looked over the top of her head at Ron. "Thanks, Schultz, for watching Andie while she went out."

Ron's eyes cracked open. He held her gaze and refused to look away. Finally, he broke eye contact and smiled at Tanner. "No problem, boss."

As they drove, Andie stared out the window. She narrowed her eyes when she saw some homeless men huddled together on benches in a downtown park. The limo passed alleyways where some were gathered around a burning barrel, their breath forming tiny vapor clouds in the brisk afternoon air. The homeless occupied doorways, their hands cupped as they begged passing pedestrians for money.

"Tanner?"

She felt his lips stir against her hair. "Hmmm?"

"Where is the nearest shelter?"

"The battered women's shelter is over—"

"No, the homeless shelter."

"Why?"

Andie turned in his arms and looked up at him. "Why are there so many homeless around here?"

Ron made a disgusted half-sigh, half-snort. "I *know*. They're all over. They come out of the woodwork like roaches, and they're just as difficult to get rid of."

"What'd you say?" Andie asked.

Tanner settled his hand on her knee. He squeezed it. In warning? Or reassurance?

Ron bent his head and studied his buffed nails. "Why do you care?"

"Why don't you?"

"Why should I? They bring it on themselves."

"Some of those people are more educated than you, Ron!"

"Then why don't they get off the streets, if they're so smart?"

"Some have just had a hard time in life and—"

"Cool it, both of you," Tanner said.

"Isn't anything being done to help these people?"

"There isn't enough room at the shelter for them," Tanner said. "Two shelters have closed this year because of lack of funding. There just isn't enough to go around."

"They need to get jobs," Ron said. "If it wasn't for them—"

"What?" Andie said, leaning forward in her seat.

Tanner must have thought she was going to go after Ron because he grabbed her elbow and pulled her against him.

"You try living out there, Ron, and see how long you survive!" Andie said. "You wouldn't make it one night."

Ron lifted his eyebrows. "And you would?"

"I—"

Tanner silenced her with a squeeze of his hand.

I did for almost ten years, she almost said.

"Let's forget this and just go home, okay?" Tanner brushed Andie's bangs away and dropped an affectionate kiss on her forehead.

Andie opened her mouth to say something but Tanner lifted his hand and touched her lips to silence her. She suddenly became aware of Ron and turned to see his eyes narrowed in suspicion as he watched them.

~ Eighteen ~

The next morning, Ron knocked on Tanner's office door.

"It's open."

Ron stepped inside and shut the door. "Andie let me upstairs."

Tanner lifted his head from where he was hunched over his desk, studying some paperwork in a manila folder. "What do you need?"

Ron walked closer and peered down at the paperwork. "What's that?"

Tanner closed the folder and pushed it away. "The budget for next year. It's depressing."

"Do you have time to talk?"

Tanner swept his hand toward the empty chair in front of his desk. "Sit. Please."

Instead of sitting, Ron remained standing and withdrew the morning newspaper from under his arm. He unfolded it and placed it on the desk. "Did you see this morning's headline?" He pushed it across the desk and leaned a hip against the desk.

Tanner pulled the newspaper closer. The large headline on the front read, *"Governor Welcomes Home Long-Lost Wife."* Below the headline was a seductive picture of him and Andie in the limousine, Andie on his lap, her arms entwined around his neck, her lips meshed against his.

Tanner looked up. "What about it?"

Ron pushed away from the desk and walked to the window. "What do you mean, what about it? What do you think that will do to your reputation? What will people think after seeing that, their governor acting that way?"

"It's a passionate kiss shared by two people who haven't seen each other in ten years."

"It's humiliating!"

"To who? You?" Tanner leaned back in his chair. "Because I don't care what people think."

Ron spun around and glared at Tanner. "Well, you should care! It might ruin your chance of being re-elected!"

Tanner slowly drew to his feet. "Is that all you care about? The damn election?"

"It's my job to care. Someone needs to, because you obviously don't!"

"This isn't about the election, is it? It's about Andie. Tell me what you really came here to say."

"It's her lack of discretion."

"If you're referring to that picture in the paper, then you have it wrong, Ron. Andie did that to settle a grudge. I deserved what I got."

"She humiliated us!"

"She humiliated you, not me."

"You should be more concerned about your image. Things will be said once people see that picture," Ron said. "That kiss—"

"Is none of your business!"

"Everything about you is my business, Tanner! Without me, you—"

"You better watch what you say, Ron. You're treading on dangerous ground."

"All I'm saying is that she needs to be taught how to act like a governor's wife. Look at how she acts and dresses. Listen to how she speaks!"

"And that embarrasses you, doesn't it?"

"It should embarrass *you*! You *are* her husband!" Ron sank into the chair across from Tanner. He leaned forward and clasped his hands together. "Governor, I've been looking into it. I know this lady, she owns a school of etiquette and I thought—"

"I won't subject my wife to etiquette classes!"

"Well, something needs to be done. The public is demanding to see her. What will they think when they see her dressed like some kind of..."

"Some kind of what?"

Ron dropped his head and closed his eyes. He squeezed his temples and said, "A governor's wife cannot go around cursing and acting like a heathen. We need to curb her tongue and her manners."

"No. No way. She doesn't need it."

"Your fund-raiser is in a few days. She needs to be presentable before then."

Tanner closed his eyes.

"Did you forget all about it?"

"No, it just...slipped my mind."

"How could you forget about it? It's your biggest fund-raiser of the year! Your whole re-election depends on it!"

"You don't have to tell me, Ron," Tanner replied. "I know."

"You have been preparing your speech, haven't you?"

Tanner didn't reply.

"Do you want this or not?"

"I do."

"Then you don't have much choice. Andra needs to learn some etiquette or it might mean the end of your governorship this year." He saw Tanner clench his jaw and before the Governor could reply, added, "What aren't you telling me?"

"What do you mean?"

"About Andra. What is it that you don't want me to know?"

"Nothing!"

"There's something you're keeping from me," Ron said.

"Something you don't want to get out."

"You're being paranoid."

"A person in your position can't have secrets," Ron said, "because they *will* be exposed. It's better to come clean. Perhaps then we can deal with it out in the open."

Tanner folded his arms. "Did you need anything else? Because as you said, I need to get ready for this fundraiser."

"Was she using drugs?"

"No."

"Was she having an affair? Was she found with her lover? Is that where she's been all these years?"

"Your imagination is quite amazing, Schultz."

"Was she hooking?"

"She was not a prostitute!"

"Then what is it?"

"It's nothing," Tanner said.

"I'm just doing my job, Governor. I'm trying to hold all of this together because I feel like it's going to blow up in our faces."

"I'm not keeping anything from you."

"Then where'd she come from?" Ron asked. "She said she had amnesia. Where did you find her?"

"Detroit."

"Detroit? Why was she in Detroit?"

"There was an accident after her abduction. She was taken to the hospital and suffered amnesia."

"And?"

"And what?"

"And then what?"

Someone suddenly knocked on the door, breaking the tension in the room.

"Who is it?" Tanner snapped.

The door cracked opened and Andie peeked inside. "I can come back later."

Ron saw the way Tanner's face softened. His boss jumped to his feet like an awkward schoolboy and said, "Come on in, sweetheart. Ron was just leaving."

Ron grabbed the newspaper off Tanner's desk. He folded it again and tucked it under his arm before turning around. He brushed by Andie without a word. The door shut abruptly behind him.

As he walked quickly down the hall, he pulled his cell phone off his belt clip and punched in Elizabeth Van Dyke's number. She answered on the second ring.

"Hello, Liz?" Ron said, hurrying outside to his car.

"Ron?"

Ron slipped inside his BMW and started the car. The car purred so softly it was difficult to tell if it was even running.

"Liz, I need you to do a background check. I want everything. Finances. Criminal history, everything."

Ron had requested this favor dozens of times before. New employees. Opponents. Everybody had been under Ron's scrutiny at one time or another.

"On whom?"

"Andra Thornburg," he replied, filling her in on the details.

~ Nineteen ~

Andie closed the door and leaned against it. "What was that about?"

"Nothing. Just business, as usual." Tanner patted his lap. "Come here."

Andie walked across the room and stopped in front of him. He reached up and pulled her down until she was sitting on his lap. He pushed her hair away. "Much better. I can actually run my hands through it again." Tanner wrapped a strand of hair around his finger. "What did you need?"

Andie leaned against him. "I was wondering if you had ever thought about doing something about the homeless."

"We can only do so much. We only have so much funding for it and times are tough lately. The damn budget cuts…" His lips sought and found her earlobe and circled the delicate flesh before his teeth nipped it lightly.

Andie leaned back, away from his wandering lips. "Would I be able to do something about it?"

Tanner lowered his head and kissed her collarbone.

"Tanner!" Lifting her hands, she cupped his face and brought it up until he was looking into her eyes. "Aren't you hearing a word I say?"

"Of course. What is it that you want to do about it?"

"Other wives use their influence to help with education or the environment or—"

"And what do you want to do?"

"If the state doesn't have funding for the homeless, why can't we raise the funds?"

"How?"

"All kinds of things. We could do walk-a-thons or car washes or—"

"I don't think it's a good idea, Andie," Tanner said.

Andie wrapped her arms around his neck and began kissing it. "But I think I could really help, Tanner." Her lips traveled up his neck to his earlobe, nipping it playfully before delving inside the shell of his ear. "I could agree to those interviews that everyone's been bugging you about as a way to get word out."

She heard him softly groan before he ripped his head away. "No, absolutely not. You aren't going in front of the cameras. And no amount of foreplay will change my mind."

Andie grinned mischievously and lowered her hand to his shirt collar. Her fingers began unbuttoning his shirt, so quickly he didn't even realize it until her lips found his Adam's apple.

"I'm not going to change my mind, Andie."

She pulled her hands away. "But why? And who says I can't? *You?* I'm not some thirteen-year-old girl that you can order around!"

"I don't want you to feel uncomfortable in any way."

"It's for a good cause. I really want to do this."

"I don't think it's a good idea."

Andie climbed off his lap. "You're being selfish! You're

just like Ron ... all you think about is yourself and your re-election. Can't you, for once, think about others instead of yourself?"

Tanner pushed the chair away from his desk and turned toward her. "I'm not going to jeopardize your safety!"

"Is it Ron? Did he say something to you about me? Is that why you both looked pissed when I knocked?"

"Andie..." Tanner reached out but she sidestepped him. "Please. Just come here for a minute and let's talk about this."

"Did you tell him about me? About my history?"

"No."

"Why not? You're embarrassed, aren't you?"

"I'm protecting you. You've been through so much already. I didn't want to put you through more. That's why I don't want you going on camera."

"You're protecting *you*," she said, folding her arms across her chest, leaning against the bookshelves. "You're afraid it'll—that *I'll*—ruin your chances of re-election."

"Who told you that? Ron?"

"Nobody had to tell me. I'm not stupid."

"It's not true." He lifted his hands, his fingers waggling at her. "Andie, will you please come over here?"

Andie didn't move. "Ron and Elizabeth don't even know. Why haven't you told them?"

"I'll tell them when it's the right time."

"When is the right time?"

"I don't know. When the opportunity comes up."

"You can't hide from it," Andie said. "Might as well confront it."

"I know that!"

"Then why are you waiting?"

He didn't reply. He turned his head and wouldn't look at her. But she already knew the answer. It was because he was embarrassed and afraid of what it would do to his reputation.

"Can I at least go down to the shelter on Christmas Eve to help serve food to the homeless?"

"I don't see a problem with that. As long as security—"
His eyes widened. "Oh. Wait. That's not going to work."
"Why not?"
"There's a holiday party that night I need to attend. I need you there with me."
"Holiday party? On Christmas Eve? What's it for?"
He cleared his throat. "A fund-raiser. For my campaign. I had forgotten all about it."
"On Christmas Eve? Who plans something like that on Christmas Eve? What about all those families who are getting ready to celebrate with their kids—"
"It's early. Four o'clock. Plenty of time to get home. And everyone is required to bring a present for Toys for Tots. Ron says it will boost my ratings—"
"And *that's* what's important, isn't it?" Before he could reply, she walked out of the room and slammed the door behind her.

~ Twenty ~

Tanner sat across from Ron and Elizabeth in the conference room off the downstairs lobby. He folded his arms and looked up at the clock. It was nearly one o'clock in the afternoon. He still needed to prepare for the holiday party that night.
"What is so important that I had to be called in during my lunch hour? I was Christmas shopping for my wife!"
"We're sorry we interrupted you, sir," Elizabeth said. "But we felt this was important."
"It better be," Tanner said. "Christmas is tomorrow and I still don't have anything for her."
"Well, that's why we called you here, Governor," Ron said. "It's regarding Andra."
"What about her? Did something happen? Is she all right?"
Ron looked at Elizabeth and hesitated. "We know about her, Governor."

"Know about what?"

"Why didn't you tell us she had a criminal record?"

"Why was it any of your business? And who do you think you are, going behind my back and—"

"You wouldn't tell me anything." Ron spread his hands in an innocent gesture. "I felt it was in our best interests—"

"In your best interests."

Ron cleared his throat. "I felt it was wise so that when we approach the campaign this spring, we know exactly what we're dealing with. I don't want any surprises."

"It doesn't excuse what you did."

"What if the public gets a hold of this information?" Ron picked up the thick folder of information he had requested from Elizabeth. Its innards held Andie's life. Her finances. Criminal record. Medical background.

"It was easy for me to find this information," Ron said. "You don't think that the press or your opponents could do the same?"

"The public is demanding to know what happened to her, where she came from," Elizabeth said. "I field their calls on a daily basis and frankly I agree with Ron, Governor. Something needs to be done about this."

"What do you suggest?"

"Her record was under another name—Andie Petersen—and she had no known social security number. The only reason I found it was because I knew where she had come from and what hospital she had been brought to after the accident and from there..." Ron trailed off. "Well, let's just say, anybody could do the same, given the basic details."

"We could erase all this," Elizabeth said. "Make it go away."

Ron nodded. "I have connections."

"And then? When people go to look up this information, and they can't find it? What rumors will spread then?" Tanner replied. "It'll be better if we come right out and admit it."

Ron slapped the table. "Are you crazy? Have you completely lost your mind? Do you forget how it is during campaigns? The mud slinging, the dirty politics. If this gets into the wrong hands, it will not only mean the end of your governorship but possibly the end of your career. Do you want that?"

Tanner didn't reply.

Ron looked at Elizabeth. "Perhaps we should reconsider having Andra go to the holiday party tonight."

Tanner straightened. "Absolutely not. I am not ashamed of my wife!"

Ron opened the folder. "Have you seen her background?"

Tanner glanced at the clock again. "I only checked her medical background to see if she had really suffered a head injury, like she claimed."

Ron picked up the paper on top of the pile. "Do you know what it says here? Maybe if you did, you'd rethink having anything to do with her, especially at this time." He pulled the open folder onto his lap. "Says here Andra has had over thirty-three run-ins with the police. Twelve for pickpocketing, seventeen for shoplifting—"

"She had to survive on the streets," Tanner replied. "The food—"

"Not everything she shoplifted was food, Governor," Ron said, running his finger down the criminal record. "It says here … medicine, jewelry, clothes."

"Clothes. See?" Tanner's brow lifted.

Ron looked up. "Jewelry?"

Tanner climbed to his feet and hurried toward the door, reaching for the doorknob. "I'm not going to listen to this."

"Two tickets for prostitution," Ron said.

Tanner stiffened before striding out the door.

Elizabeth turned to Ron. "*Prostitution?* What if that got out?"

"Pray it doesn't." Ron closed the folder and returned it to his briefcase. "I've never seen Tanner like this. He's usually so driven and focused. I've never seen him so … distracted."

"It's her."

"I know. And we need to do something about it before she ruins everything for him."

"What do you suggest?"

"If he won't leave her, we need to convince her to leave him."

~~~~

Something was wrong.

Andie glanced at Tanner out of the corner of her eye as they rode together to the Hilton, the site of the holiday party. Wet snow stuck against the window briefly before dripping away. Christmas lights glowed from every store front.

Tanner hadn't spoken to her since his meeting that afternoon with Ron and Elizabeth. He hadn't complimented her on her dress. He wouldn't even look at her.

She glanced down at her midnight-blue evening gown. The bodice, made up of silver sequins, was complimented by silver jewelry and silver shoes.

She had gone out of her way to look nice tonight. She frowned. Maybe it was the silver heels. Were they too much for this evening?

That morning she had vowed to behave tonight. She wanted to show Tanner that she could conduct herself like a lady, that he could trust her. Maybe if she did, he would change his mind about her campaigning for the homeless.

She reached over and picked off a piece of lint from his black wool coat. "You're awfully quiet tonight."

He shifted away. It was nothing too noticeable but Andie had developed keen senses from living on the street.

"What's wrong?"

He glanced out the window as the Rockefeller Center appeared in the distance. "Nothing."

Andie rolled her eyes. "You're acting like a woman. Now do I have to pry it out of you or what?"

He looked over quickly and she saw … was that rage or

hurt in his eyes?

"Listen, I don't want to suffer any more through this damn party than I already have to. Now tell me what's wrong."

"You lied to me."

Andie's forehead furrowed. "Lied about what?"

"You. Being a prostitute."

"Being a what?"

He looked at her again, over his shoulder. "You heard what I said, Andra."

So now it was back to Andra.

"I—"

"If you're lying about that, what else are you lying about? What else don't I know?"

"How'd you know about the prostitution?"

He clenched his jaw. "So it is true."

"What else did Ron tell you about me?"

"Everything. Your criminal record."

"I thought you knew about it."

"I knew your medical background. I didn't know—maybe I didn't *want* to know—more."

"Do you believe it? The prostitution thing?"

"You say that like it's no big deal."

"The *alleged* prostitution charge is—"

"It's down in black and white, Andra," Tanner said. "How can you expect me not to believe it?"

Andie leaned against the seat. "It's not true."

"Sure."

"You don't understand, Tanner. You will *never* understand."

"You're right. I don't."

"You don't know what I went through. What it was like living out there, on the streets. What it's like wondering where you'll get your next meal, where you'll find your next place to sleep!"

"Obviously you found ways to survive, even if it meant selling your body!"

"You don't know what it's like to have those bastards pull

up to the curb, wave their badges and frisk you for drugs or weapons. They assume because you're homeless, that you're also a thief or a prostitute."

"We're almost there," Tanner said, as the limousine started to slow down.

The car rolled to a stop in front of the Hilton. Tanner opened the door to step onto the curb but Andie grabbed his wrist. He glared at her over his shoulder but sank back into the car.

"What?"

"It *is* down on my record that I was ticketed for prostitution. I won't deny it. But I want you to know, here and now, that it's not true."

"Is this another lie I'm supposed to believe?"

"Believe what you want," she said, "but know this—when you live on the streets, some cops will find any reason to harass you. And they'll use any trumped up charge just to get you in trouble. Loitering. Soliciting. Prostitution." She ticked them off on her fingers. "According to the Detroit police, I'm supposedly guilty of them all."

Some were true—the shoplifting and pickpocketing charges. She remembered an incident in Kmart a few years ago. She had been caught shoplifting over-the-counter medicine that she had swiped to try to beat a flu-like bug that had lingered for more than two weeks. The officer who had arrived to the shoplifting call had caught her admiring a necklace in the jewelry department—with the medicine in her pocket. He had automatically assumed he had caught her red-handed, getting ready to stick the necklace in her other pocket. Her mistake had been not leaving the store when she'd had the chance.

The manager had not pressed charges after Andie agreed to pay for it with what little money she had.

"Andie, the press is coming and if you—"

"Don't worry, Tanner," she said. "I won't embarrass you tonight, if that's what you're worried about. I'll be the perfect, docile politician's wife because I know how important this thing is to you tonight."

More important than me, she wanted to add but didn't as she stepped out to face the press.

~ Twenty-One ~

"Julia, did you see that dress the governor's wife is wearing tonight? Good gracious, silver *sequins*? It looks like something my daughter would wear at the prom."

"I think it's quite elegant, Annabelle," another woman exclaimed.

Andie stiffened as she reached for the ladle resting inside the punch bowl. It clicked noisily against the crystal bowl as she served herself some punch. The women probably couldn't see her around the large ice sculpture positioned beside the food table in the back of the room. If they had, they probably wouldn't be speaking so candidly.

"I heard that she's not quite right," the deeper voice of Julia said, "you know…in the head."

"What happened to her, do you think?"

"I don't know. They're keeping it *very* hush-hush."

"I think I would too if my wife mysteriously appeared after ten years. They thought she was dead all these years."

"If indeed it *is* Andra Thornburg."

"You don't think it is?"

"It's quite convenient, don't you think? Showing up right before re-election?"

"You think it's another ploy to win votes, like before?"

"Most definitely. Don't you?"

Andie backed away from the table, held her punch tightly in her trembling hands and walked around the ice sculpture to face her accusers. They stood, posed in front of the ice sculpture, scanning the crowd.

One woman turned her head and glanced at Andra. Her eyebrows lifted and she covered her shock with a smile that showed off perfect white teeth.

"Mrs. Thornburg, hello. How are you tonight? It's

wonderful to see you here." She didn't look much older than Andie. Black hair was piled on her head with ringlets falling softly against her face. She wore a strapless aqua dress that hugged her curves and fell gracefully to the floor.

It was a brave woman who wore aqua anything, Andie thought, as she returned the smile. "Hello."

The other woman beside her smiled. "I just *love* your dress. Where did you get it?"

Andie forced a smile and resisted the urge to throw the contents of her glass on the woman's flesh-colored evening gown. It might give her some color, Andie thought, running her eyes down the woman's too-thin body. The woman looked positively colorless and gaunt in that dress. She opened her mouth to reply with a cunning remark but felt a hand curl around her elbow. She turned to see Ron Schultz.

"Hello, ladies." Ron lifted his wineglass. "Beautiful night tonight, isn't it?"

"Beautiful." The woman in the flesh-colored dress extended her hand toward Andie. "Julia Masterson. Jeffrey Masterson's wife."

Andie racked her brain. Should she know Jeffrey Masterson?

The woman frowned. "Jeff is the Lieutenant Governor," Julia said.

Andie accepted the handshake. "How do you do?"

Julia looked at Ron. "Mr. Schultz, how are you this fine evening?"

"Very well, thank you, Julia. And how is the Lieutenant Governor?"

Julia lifted her head and glanced across the room at a man standing next to Tanner, talking rapidly and gesturing wildly. "Very well, thank you." She turned to her friend. "Andra, this is Annabelle Amenson, the Secretary of State's wife."

Andie shook Annabelle's hand and then returned her attention to the glass of punch clasped in her hand.

"Is this your first party since being back?" Annabelle asked.

"Uh, yes." There was a moment of awkward silence. Andie looked around for Tanner, wishing he'd come over and save her.

Julia leaned closer. "So, Andra—"

"Call me Andie."

"Andie, everybody wants to know ... where have you been all these years?"

Ron's grasp tightened around her elbow. "You know what? I see someone I'd like to introduce Andra to, if you don't mind."

Andie pulled her elbow out of his grasp and met Julia's cold blue eyes. "You wouldn't believe it even if I told you."

"What was Tanner's reaction when he found you?" Annabelle asked. "He must have been surprised."

"Oh," Andie said, her eyes widening, "shocked is more like it."

Julia stepped forward and lowered her voice. "Where did he find you? I mean, what have you been doing all these years? Why didn't you come home sooner?"

"Ladies, I believe the governor will begin his speech soon," Ron said, pulling Andie away. "It's so nice of you to come tonight and it's been a pleasure to talk with you."

Julia stiff smile dropped. "Yes, a pleasure."

Ron hurried Andie away. "Well, that was a catastrophe nicely averted, wouldn't you say?"

Andie stopped suddenly and yanked her elbow out of his tight grasp. "You don't have to worry, Ron. I'll keep your precious secret."

"It's not you I'm worried about."

Andie turned to a table covered with food. Barbecued chicken wings, vegetable dips, fruits, salads, rolls, casseroles and more. Enough to feed the homeless at the shelter, she thought, wishing she was there instead.

Ron plucked a piece of broccoli off the vegetable tray and dunked it in a cream-colored dip before popping it in his mouth. "I bet you haven't seen this much food in your lifetime?

I mean, being homeless and all."

She grabbed a plate and began piling fruit on it. "You're a bastard, Ron. I only wish Tanner knew how much."

Ron leaned his hip against the table. He bent over from the waist until his breath stirred her hair as he whispered, "I must say you've surprised me tonight, Andra. You're actually acting like a lady instead of the two-bit whore you are."

Andie saw her hands were shaking as she broke open a roll to butter it. He was goading her. Only trying to provoke a fight in public. She wouldn't allow him the satisfaction. She turned away and walked toward the door that led to the balcony outside, hoping the cold December night would deter him from following her.

It didn't.

She felt his presence behind her as she stepped outside on the balcony. A layer of snow covering the wide balcony lay undisturbed.

"You're a pig," she said, wishing for a shawl or something to put around her shoulders. She shivered as she brought the roll to her mouth and in the middle of chewing her food, mumbled, "I don't know why Tanner keeps you."

"Because he can't afford to lose me." Ron turned toward her and leaned against the railing. She could smell the whiskey on his breath. "This re-election means everything to him and he needs his full concentration to get through the roughest months ahead."

"I know that and I support him."

Lifting his hand, he fingered a shoulder strap, his fingers rasping against the silky material. "You're cold. You have goose bumps." His fingers slipped off the strap and touched her bare shoulder.

Andie ripped her shoulder from his touch. "Don't touch me."

"According to your criminal record, you like men touching you."

"I think you should leave."

Ron stepped closer until he was nestled against her body. She refused to move away, to give him the satisfaction of knowing that he intimidated her. Narrowing her eyes, she glared at him, silently daring him to touch her again.

He did. He drew his fingers down between her breasts, down her belly and—

"You're drunk Ron."

Andie stepped away, breaking contact. She turned to go but he grabbed her arm. The sudden movement caused her to drop the plate; strawberries, blueberries and chunks of pineapple landed at her feet. She didn't know what to do. Tanner would never believe her.

"Come on, Andra." Ron yanked her against him. "You put out for others, but you won't put out for me?"

Andie's hands splayed against his chest. "Let me go, you pervert!"

"Playing hard to get?" He grabbed her waist and trailed his fingers up her ribs until his hand was inches from her breast.

Andie pushed his hand away and struggled to uncurl the fingers that held her elbow like a vise. "Let me go, Ron!"

"Money. Isn't that what you're holding out for?" He shoved her into the back corner of the dark balcony, out of view from the guests inside. She struggled to keep her balance as his hands groped her but her heels only slid in the snow. She tried to push him away at the same time she tried to regain her footing to run but before she could, his lips were on hers. He mashed his lips against hers, trying to force her to open her mouth.

She managed to rip her head away to scream once before his tongue slipped inside. But she went unheard over the booming microphone as someone asked Tanner to come up to the front of the room.

Ron fumbled with her zipper.

"Get away from me!" She pushed at his chest but he was a solid force against her. She had nowhere to go. She opened her mouth to scream but he clamped a hand over it and met her eyes.

"Come on, Andra. I know you want this." He lowered his hand to his pants and she heard leather slap against leather as he undid his belt.

She thrashed against him. Her fists beat against his chest and shoulders as her muffled cries went unheard against his hand.

As Ron ripped his dress shirt from his pants, she sank her teeth into his palm at the same time she raised her knee to drive it into his groin. He averted her knee and only succeeded in angering him. He raised his hand to slap her but she saw it coming and turned her head. Ron's blow missed her face but struck her ear and she cried out from the stinging pain.

Ron grimaced, looking down at his palm. "You bit me. I can't believe you bit me!" He clenched and unclenched his hand. "Bit me like the bitch in heat you are!"

She used that moment to slip past him and run for the doors. Swinging them open, she charged into the room. A few startled guests glanced at her in surprise as she raced past them and into the lobby.

~ Twenty-Two ~

When the balcony doors burst open, Tanner was standing on the dais, preparing to give his speech. He looked up to see his wife blow through, her eyes wild, her hair wilder, torn apart by the wind. She slipped on the tiled floor, almost falling before she regained her footing and rushed from the room.

Tanner signaled the band to start playing Christmas music as he climbed off the dais.

His speech was forgotten. The only thing on his mind was his wife. What was wrong? What had happened?

He saw no sign of her as he entered the lobby. Several women glanced at him curiously as they stood in a line outside the bathroom door.

"Merry Christmas, Governor Thornburg," one of them said.

Someone brushed against him. He looked down to see Ron.

"Ron, did you see what happened? Did you see where she went?"

Ron hurried to catch up with Tanner as he crossed the lobby. "I don't know, sir. I—I saw two women talking to her a few minutes ago. Maybe they said something inappropriate."

"It wasn't hurt I saw on her face." Tanner pushed the revolving doors and emerged on the other side. He was hit by a sudden burst of winter air. "It was fear."

"Fear, sir?"

Tanner looked left and right but could see nothing through the wall of people hurrying by as they did last minute Christmas shopping.

Jared McPherson appeared beside him. "Sir, what happened, sir? I was patrolling the lobby when Andie came barreling through that door and—"

"Did you see where she went?"

"She climbed in a cab and sped off before I could stop her," Jared replied, stiffening as people on the sidewalks began recognizing Tanner. Several of them slowed and stared as they walked past. Some pointed. Others wished him a Merry Christmas.

"Did you see what direction she went?" Tanner asked.

"Sir, we should probably get back into the hotel, away from the crowd," he said.

"Did you see where she went, Jared?"

Jared pointed. "That way, sir. Would you like me to send someone home to meet her? Make sure she gets home all right?"

"But home is in the other direction," Ron said.

"That won't be necessary," Tanner said. "She's not going home."

"Where is she going then?" Ron asked.

Tanner looked at Jared. "Jared, if you could send the limo around, I'll need a ride—"

"But, sir!" Ron's eyes widened. "You can't leave! Not with all of these people here on your behalf! They are funding your election!"

Jared's cell phone chirped as he two-wayed the limousine driver and instructed him to meet them in the front of the Hilton.

Tanner glanced at his watch. "Some things are more important, Ron."

"But, sir, you don't even know where she went! Now just come back inside—"

"I know exactly where she went," Tanner said, as the limousine pulled up in front of them.

Jared climbed into the front seat, Tanner into the back. He barked directions and sat back as the limousine took off.

~~~~

"Am I too late to help?"

The woman looked up from where she was bent over the table, scribbling a grocery list. "No, we're just starting." Her long hair was steel gray but her face suggested a younger woman. Her bright blue eyes rivaled the sweater she was wearing.

"Good. What can I do to help?" Andie glanced around the large room that served as a dining area. It was bright and smelled like lemon, probably from the cleaning supplies they used. Several long tables were pushed together, covered with forest-green table clothes. Red poinsettias were centered on each table. A Christmas tree, in its full splendor, decorated, sat in the corner of the room. Flashing bulbs shot red, yellow and blue splashes against the walls.

Andie hugged her discarded dress and shoes against her chest. She had been worried that the brief stop at the department store to purchase jeans, a sweater and athletic shoes would delay her from getting to the homeless shelter in time. She couldn't show up wearing this dress. Nobody would take her seriously. She would be accused of doing this for publicity.

"Paul in back needs some…" The woman became silent and began tapping her pen against the notepad. "Oh. Oh my. You—you're her. I mean, you're Andra Thornburg, the governor's wife. I just saw your picture in the paper."

"Where would you like me, ma'am?"

The woman climbed to her feet and held out her hand. "Martha Dexter. I run the homeless shelter. May I ask why you're here, Mrs. Thornburg?"

"Call me Andie, please. And I'm here to help."

Martha pursed her lips. "Why?" She glanced over Andie's shoulder at the front door as if she expected the press to enter at any moment. "If you've come for some kind of publicity, I'm afraid you've come to the wrong place, madam."

"I came on my own accord, Ms. Dexter."

"Where's your husband? Did he put you up to this?"

Andie fingered the collar of her gown. "My husband doesn't even know I'm here."

A long moment of silence passed before Martha lowered her arms to her side. "I believe you."

"I came on my own."

"On Christmas Eve?"

"Yes, ma'am."

Martha picked up the grocery list. "Well then. Let's get you started."

Andie followed her into the kitchen and was overcome by the smell of baking bread. Fresh bread. How lucky to have fresh bread. The only bread she had eaten on the streets was stale bread that had reached its expiration date, donated by area grocery stores.

Everybody looked up as she entered, their jobs momentarily forgotten. A woman stirring soup dropped the spoon she was using to measure salt. A man in the middle of pulling bread from the oven looked up.

Martha smiled. "Excuse me, everyone. We have a new helper I'd like you to meet."

Everyone looked at her. Some in surprise. Others in suspicion.

Andie clasped her hands behind her back. She only wanted

to help. She didn't have a hidden motive for being here.

One man stepped forward. "You're Andra Thornburg." He wiped his hands on a towel and leaned against the counter. "You're the governor's wife."

"Yes, sir." Andie lowered her eyes to the nametag that was pinned to his shirt. "I'm here to help in any way I can, Mr. Bishop."

"Why?" he asked.

"Paul!" Martha cried.

Paul Bishop met Martha's eyes. He was a handsome man, Andie thought. Tall. Blond. Well-dressed. A full, well-groomed beard. He spoke with a slight southern accent as he asked, "Why are you here?"

"Yeah, why aren't you at the holiday party? I heard on the news that it was tonight." The woman preparing the soup asked. Her nametag read Eileen Bishop. Paul Bishop's wife?

"I left it to come here." Andie thought she would find a warm, inviting atmosphere here. Friendly, caring people who, like her, were concerned about others. Perhaps she had made a mistake.

She wasn't going anywhere. They were the ones mistaken. She wanted to be accepted for who she was, not what she was. She wanted to help and felt hurt at being treated this way.

"You left the party to come here?" Paul ripped off the oven mitt he had used to take the pan from the oven. "You want to spend your Christmas Eve here, tonight? With us?"

"I thought you could use an extra pair of hands."

A new expression passed through the room: one of respect.

Paul stepped forward and clapped a hand on her shoulder. "Well, then, let's find you something to do before the crowd gets here." He handed her a box of plastic gloves. "Put these on. You can help serve soup tonight."

~ Twenty-Three ~

Tanner stood in the doorway. Unbuttoning his coat, he looked around the room. It was crowded and difficult to see past the line of men, women and...

Children.

There were children in line, waiting for food. Some looked no older than two or three.

My God, he thought. He had never really thought that children could be homeless too. In fact, he hadn't thought much about the homeless before, he admitted.

Everyone was in good spirits despite the hard life they lived. One older woman was at the piano, playing Christmas music. Others were gathered around her, singing.

Men were hunched over the tables, talking. Others held children on their laps. Nobody seemed to notice him yet.

Or maybe they just didn't care.

As Tanner walked closer, he saw Andie serving soup to a man. She handed him a bowl of what looked like chicken noodle soup. She smiled, leaned closer and laughed at something he had said. The corners of her eyes lifted at whatever joke he'd just told.

Tanner slowed on his way across the room. When had she laughed, really laughed, like that with him? He couldn't recall seeing her eyes turn up at something he had said or done. He couldn't remember her laughing much, really.

He pulled off his leather gloves and shoved them in his pockets. The truth hit him almost as hard as the blast of winter air that entered the shelter as another family slipped inside.

Andie was unhappy. But was she unhappy because of him, or the life he lived?

As he walked closer, he saw her lips moving but nobody was around her. When he stopped before her, he realized she was quietly singing along to the music as she stirred the soup.

"Hello, Andie."

Looking up, her eyes widened. "Tanner!" She opened her mouth to say more but a man edged past Tanner and reached for a bowl of soup. Andie reached down and handed it to him.

"Thank you, Miss Andie," he said before walking to an empty table.

Tanner's gaze followed the man. "I see that everyone is already well-acquainted with you."

"Martha introduced me to everyone earlier. Everyone here is really nice."

Tanner lifted a brow. "Martha?"

"Martha Dexter. She runs the place." Andie looked over her shoulder. "She's right over … she just ducked into the kitchen."

Andie grabbed a towel, dabbing at soup that had spilled on the table. "Tanner, what are you doing here?" She ran her eyes down his tuxedo. "Somebody might see you."

"Andie, I—"

Jared McPherson appeared at Tanner's side. Ripping off his gloves, he glared at his boss. "Sir, I can't have you running off. The car didn't even come to a stop before you…" Jared stopped talking as everyone in the dining area turned to look at them. The music stopped and the singers looked over their shoulders at Tanner.

"Who's that in the tux up there?" he heard one man whisper to another.

"That's the governor, you idiot!" came the whispered reply.

"Maybe we should take off," somebody else said. "I don't want no trouble."

Tanner frowned and glanced around the room. How could there be trouble? And then he realized that the looks from the dining area weren't in respect. They were suspicion and fear.

Tanner rested a hand on Jared's shoulder. "You can leave, Jared. I'll be fine."

"Sir, I can't—"

"Jared, I'll be fine." Tanner lowered his voice as he said, "Take off early tonight and enjoy Christmas Eve with your family."

"Your safety could be jeopardized here."

Tanner could see Andie looking at him from the corner of his eye. He turned, met her gaze, realized she was waiting for him to relent.

"Jared—"

"I'm not leaving, sir."

Tanner sighed. "Wait in the limo, if you must stay."

Jared backed away and zipped his coat. "Yes, sir."

Tanner turned to Andie. "Andie, I—"

"Tanner, you're embarrassing me," she whispered, stirring the soup. "I've just started to earn their trust and then you come in here with your tux and your guard and scare everyone half to death!"

"I only wanted to make sure you were all right." He slipped out of his coat. "You left the party in such a hurry."

"I'm fine. Now could you please leave? We have food to serve."

Tanner unbuttoned his cuffs and rolled up his shirtsleeves. "I want to help."

"Tanner, you don't have to."

"I want to." Tanner glanced at the other individuals serving the food. "Now how can I help?"

Martha Dexter stepped forward and introduced herself. "Sir, thank you for coming. We can use all the help we can get, but we need to start by getting you out of that outfit." She clasped his hand and drew him into the kitchen. "There're some clean clothes we keep here for the needy."

Andie looked over her shoulder as if she expected him to protest but he followed Martha and emerged a few minutes later, dressed in jeans and a sweater.

Martha handed Tanner a sharp bread knife. "Here, sir. You—"

"Call me Tanner, please."

"Tanner," Martha said, positioning him next to Andie. "Stand next to your wife. You can cut some bread." She shifted Tanner closer until he bumped into Andie and then she left to tend to others.

The line resumed again and Tanner carefully cut the bread and placed it on plates as they passed by. Fifteen minutes passed in silence before Andie said, "How did you know I was here?"

"Where else would you be on Christmas Eve? I knew how important this was to you."

The Nextel on Tanner's belt clip suddenly chirped to life. He turned away to answer the two-way call.

"Yes, Jared?"

"Sir, the press has caught wind of this," Jared's monotone voice filtered quietly through the Nextel. "What would you like to do?"

"Keep those vultures away. I don't want them harassing anybody here."

"Yes, sir."

The cell phone fell silent.

"What about your party?" Andie asked.

"What about it?"

"You left your party to come here?"

"I wasn't enjoying myself. How could I without you?" He touched her waist. "What happened back there, Andie? Ron told me that some of the women were harassing you."

Andie stirred the soup. "I—Ron, he…" she hesitated. "Yes. They were."

"Who was it?"

"It doesn't matter."

"It matters to me. Was it someone on my staff?"

Andie lifted her hand and placed it gently over his, touched by his concern. He was here. He had come. He cared.

After a half-hour had passed, Martha came up to them, handing each of them a paper plate. "Here. Take this and help yourself to some food. Everybody has eaten except you guys." She pointed toward an empty table in the back of the room. "Go ahead and grab a table. I can take over up here if somebody should want seconds."

Tanner accepted the paper plate. "Thanks."

Martha shooed them away. Andie and Tanner walked down the length of the table, grabbed some food and huddled together.

Tanner broke a piece of bread in half and watched Andie

sample the soup. "How is it?"

Andie closed her eyes. "Wonderful. They sure didn't have homemade soup when I was..." She stopped suddenly and looked at him.

Tanner lowered his eyes to his plate of food. "You're right, you know."

"About what?"

"I never really realized what you went through on the streets. I think I do now."

Andie reached over and squeezed his hand. "I'm glad."

Tanner shook his head as he stirred his soup. "I'm going to see if we can increase state funding for the shelters."

She looked up at him with wide eyes. "But how? I thought your budget—"

"The budget hasn't been approved yet. There's still time to juggle some stuff around."

She smiled. "Tanner, that'd be great!"

He returned her smile but it didn't quite reach his sad eyes. "You know, I walked in here and saw the children. I—I guess I didn't realize children could be affected."

"More than you know."

"I want to help if I can."

"I'll help in any way I can," she said, running her hand up his arm.

He reached in his pocket. "I almost forgot." He withdrew a small, wrapped box. "This is for you, Andie. Merry Christmas."

Andie picked up the box. "Tanner, you didn't have to."

He smiled at her and this time it was genuine. "Open it."

She tore off the paper and eyed the small white box.

"Open it, Andie," he prodded.

Taking off the top of the lid, she saw a velvet jewelry box inside. "What is it?"

"Open it and find out."

She turned the box upside down and fingered the velvet jewelry box that fell into her palm. Lifting the lid, she smiled.

A necklace. On it was—she looked closer—what appeared to be a tiny compass. It turned and gave the direction as she pointed it at different corners of the room. Tanner took it from her hands and unclasped it. "So you're never lost again." Leaning forward, he slipped it around her neck and fastened it. "Merry Christmas, sweetheart."

~ Twenty-Four ~

"Here. Let me get that, Martha." Andie took the garbage bag from Martha as the older woman struggled to pull it from the trashcan. Dragging it closer, Andie tied it tightly and looked over her shoulder. "Where does it go?"

Martha straightened and pointed toward the back kitchen door. "A dumpster out in back. But, Andie, reporters are all over outside. I can take it."

"It's no problem." Andie looked over at Tanner, who was wiping down the kitchen counters with a bottle of disinfectant clenched in one hand and a dishcloth in the other. He haggled with Paul over who was New York's strongest NHL team: the Rangers, Islanders or Sabres.

He had fit right in tonight with the others and seemed to enjoy himself. Andie watched as he leaned against the countertop and crossed his arms, laughing loudly at something Paul had said. His hands waved about, lifting and falling as he tried to describe something.

She studied his hands and imagined how they would feel against her body. Something stirred inside and for once it didn't startle her. She was beginning to develop feelings for him. Respect, yes. Pride, yes. Love? She didn't know. It was too soon.

Andie looked up to see Tanner turn his head and meet her eyes. The corners of his eyes lifted as he smiled warmly. Andie returned the smile. Paul continued to talk to him but Tanner wasn't looking at Paul anymore—he was staring at her. His smile slipped and the kindness in his eyes was replaced by a heated, intense expression that communicated what he wanted, what he was thinking, more than words ever could.

"I—I'll just be a minute, Martha." Andie's mouth was suddenly dry and she took a drink from some bottled water. Drying her mouth with the back of her hand, she leaned over and picked up the bag, walking toward the back door. As she passed Tanner, she felt his hand playfully slap her rear end. She stiffened in surprise. Looking over her shoulder, she met his eyes and saw in them a twinkle of amusement.

"Hurry back," he said, his eyebrows waggling at her suggestively.

She laughed and shook her head, pushing the garbage bag against the door to open it. She scanned the empty parking lot as the door shut behind her. It was well lit; it had to be in this neighborhood. The lights kept the shadows on a tight leash, confined to the corners of the lot. A light above the dumpster strobed in the darkness, revealing spray paint along the sides.

Being out here didn't frighten her. This paled in comparison to some of Detroit's parking lots. It was the reporters she was more scared of.

She looked around but saw no reporters or photographers. Jared and his team were doing a great job of keeping the press at bay. She could see and hear commotion from the front of the building—people shouting questions, security warning people to step back, the red and blue flash of a police cruiser parked near the curb as it kept watch.

She crossed the parking lot, dragging the heavy bag behind her. Stopping at the dumpster, she lifted the lid and gagged at the smell. It smelled like rotten food and urine.

Andie held her breath and grabbed the garbage bag, lifting it up and over the side of the huge container. She heard glass break as the bag landed inside. Lowering the lid, she turned away and wiped her hands against her pants, anxious to get back inside.

She took a step toward the building. She saw the silhouette

of a man in front of her and stopped abruptly, swallowing a gasp of surprise. Her mouth opened...what should she say?

"Uh...hi." She thought she was alone. How had she not heard him approach? "Can I help you?"

Peering closer, she noticed his face shadowed by a baseball cap. Who was he? Where had he come from? Had he come from the shelter?

Another reporter?

"Tanner? Paul, is that you?"

He lifted his hand and nudged his ball cap back, revealing his face.

"Hello, Andie."

Brian Petersen—no, Brian *Phelps*.

She could never forget him. The same boyish face. Same scar above his eye. Same full lips that some women would call sensual if they weren't twisted into a scowl all the time. Crow's feet were the only indication of time passing.

He still appeared harmless, an average Joe that nobody would suspect of kidnapping and attempted murder.

Andie backed away and felt the side of the dumpster against her back, barring her way. She folded her arms across her chest to hide shaky hands.

"What do you want, Brian? How'd you find me? How'd you get back here?" She glanced quickly around the parking lot, hoping to spot Jared or another security guard patrolling the back lot but they had their work cut out for them up front, trying to keep the reporters at bay.

She returned her gaze to Brian. She was afraid of being distracted too long; if he reacted, she might not be prepared for his attack.

"It wasn't difficult, believe me." Brian stepped forward until he was only a few feet away. "Your story is live right now, on televisions everywhere in New York. I just didn't think it'd be this easy to get you...alone."

It sounded ominous, they way he hesitated with the last word. She felt her chest tighten in response to his nearness.

He was close enough to reach out and grab her before she had a chance to get away.

"I want what I've always wanted. *You*. I've been looking for you for ten years."

"You better go while you have the chance, Brian. Security is patrolling the parking lot and it's just a matter of minutes before they make their rounds back here."

Brian laughed. "I've been watching the guards all night, Andie. I know their routine—they've been wrapped up with those reporters up front the whole night."

"All I have to do is scream and they'll come running." She opened her mouth to do so but before she could, his hands wrapped around her throat and she felt something sharp prick her collarbone.

"And all I have to do is slide this across your throat." Brian lifted the carving knife up to her face. Her own wide, terror-filled eyes reflected in the silver glint of the knife.

Brian lowered his eyes and studied her throat. She felt his fingers loosen and turn from menacing to caressing.

"Where were you all these years, Andie?" His thumb stroked her pulse point. "When I read that you had been found, I couldn't believe it. I thought you were dead. Why else wouldn't you show up in all those years?"

His fingers tightened once more. She pushed words up her constricted airway and said, "I was in Detroit. On the streets, trying to survive."

He slid the side of the knife against her snow-white skin. "It's time for a reunion, don't you think?" Andie stiffened as his lips replaced the path of the knife. His lips were slug-like as they trailed to her earlobe. He grasped her earlobe between his teeth.

"What do you want?"

He slipped his hand under her shirt and stroked her side. "It should be obvious."

She struggled to push him away, but he was like a solid wall, hardened both by exercise and time. He merely laughed at her attempt and hooked his thumb around her belt loop, drawing her closer until she was pressed against his body. She heard the whisper of leather as he undid her belt.

She vowed to kill him first.

She drove her knee up but he shifted and she missed her target.

She must have got close enough because he made a strange sound, half-gasp, half-grunt, and bent over in pain, allowing her to flee. She raced for the back door, screaming for help. She was one step away from the door when he reached her.

His arm snaked out and grabbed her, pulling her against him as she flailed at the doorknob. She managed to scream again before he placed her in a headlock and clamped his hand—smelling like grease and sweat—against her mouth.

"I'm gonna make you regret doing that!" His headlock tightened until she couldn't breathe. Andie clawed at his arm but lost strength as spots danced in front of her eyes, popping and flashing like lightning bugs, her vision narrowing. Pinpoints of light at the end of the tunnel widened, unconsciousness beckoning her. The light grew until she stopped struggling and fell to her knees.

"Now I'm going to make her pay."

"Tanner, help me." Her scream came out a whisper as she gasped for breath.

Tanner didn't hesitate as he leaped at Brian, throwing him off Andie. They rolled away, a flurry of fists. Andie slowly sat up and tried to concentrate on the two men struggling but her vision swam in and out of focus. She opened her mouth— *should she scream for help or warn Tanner about the knife?*

Andie lifted her hand to her sore throat. "Tanner… knife…." she managed to say before Brian pushed Tanner off him and stumbled away.

Brian dug at his back and emerged with a gun cupped in his hands. He clicked off the safety, settled his finger around the trigger and waved it threateningly in Tanner's face.

Tanner climbed to his feet and stepped in front of Andie, shielding her. "What are you doing, Phelps? Put the gun down before someone gets hurt."

"I'm in control here, Thornburg, not you!" Brian cried.

Tanner narrowed his eyes. "What do you want?"

"What do you think I want?"

Tanner crossed his arms. "She's not negotiable."

"She's going with me, like it or not!"

"Over my dead body!"

Brian cocked the hammer of the revolver. "If you insist."

As Andie heard the deadly, metallic snick of the weapon, fear spurt through her blood, stronger than any adrenaline. She stepped out from behind Tanner. "Don't hurt him, Brian, please! I'll come with you. Just don't hurt him, okay?"

"Andie, don't do this!" Tanner cried. "Get back, get away from him!"

Brian reached out and pulled Andie closer. "No funny stuff, Andie."

"No funny stuff. I promise. Just leave him alone."

"If you want someone for ransom, take me." Tanner stepped forward. "I'm worth twice as much as she is. Just let her go and I'll come with you."

Brian tugged Andie against him and spun her around until her back was pressing against his chest. He wrapped an arm around her throat and stepped back. "You're not quite as appealing as she is."

"Run, Tanner, *please!*" Andie said as Brian dragged her away.

When Brian turned, Tanner suddenly jumped toward him. Brian lifted the gun to pull the trigger. Andie yanked his arm down and the gun fired harmlessly. The two men went down together and rolled along the ground, wrestling for control of the gun. She saw Brian clamber to his feet and take a few steps around the building before Tanner caught him again. And then both men disappeared around the corner.

Andie backed away, pressing herself against the building. She looked wildly about. *Where was security?*

"Somebody, someone, help please!" she cried. Should

she go? Should she stay? *She didn't know!* She couldn't leave Tanner. She had to know if he would be all right and—

Another gunshot rang out. The sounds of struggle stopped. It was replaced by shouts from the security guards as they raced around the building, toward the gunshots.

"Tanner?" She opened her mouth to call out again but another gunshot went off, she wondered if it had been meant for her. Dropping to the ground, she lay there with her ear pressed against the blacktop. She lifted her head and crawled forward, peeking around the corner of the building.

Brian was on his stomach a few feet away, his arms outstretched above his head, his face turned away. He appeared dead.

"Tanner?" She looked past Brian and saw her husband sprawled on his back. "Tanner!" Her hands, her breath, trembled as she scrambled toward him and slowly rolled him over.

"Tanner? Tanner! Please answer me!"

Tanner's eyes were closed. His chest was as red as Brian's. And his face…pale and lifeless.

She knelt over him and laid her ear against his chest, she cried out in relief when she heard a faint heartbeat. Pressing her hands against the wound, she tried to stem the blood flow as she whispered, "Tanner, hang on, hang on, help's coming."

His breath was labored and wet. Had the bullet nicked his lungs or stomach?

She heard footsteps and looked up to see Jared.

"He's been shot," she said. "He needs help."

"What in God's name happened?"

"Brian. Brian came back."

He met her eyes. She saw fear in them. Tanner was more than a boss to Jared; he was also his friend.

"Go! Go get help!" she cried.

~ Twenty-Five ~

Andie gingerly touched the bandage across Tanner's forehead. His cuts and bruises were beginning to heal from his struggle with Brian. His other wound—the gunshot to his stomach—was the one that concerned her the most. The bullet had entered below his ribcage to lodge in his lower abdomen. It had nicked his liver, requiring removal of part of it to stop blood loss and save his life.

She grasped his hand and squeezed it. He was alive. That's all that mattered.

"Tanner, wake up, please."

There was no response except the hum and click of machines in the room. Dozens of flower arrangements cluttering the windowsill overpowered the smell of disinfectant. Many of Tanner's friends had stopped by to offer their prayers for recovery.

It had been nearly two days. He still hadn't regained consciousness. Christmas had come and gone.

Andie leaned over, pressing her cheek against his. She felt his stubble from days of not shaving. "Tanner, please wake up."

Glancing at the clock, she noticed the early hour. Seven o'clock.

She brushed Tanner's hair off his forehead, letting her fingers linger in the ebony strands. His handsome face, normally tanned and vital with life, was pale from lack of blood. His eyelids fluttered at her touch but never opened. He was lost in sleep, his body fighting to heal from the bullet wound.

Andie traced the blue river of veins on the back of his hand before bringing his hand to her mouth to tenderly kiss his knuckles.

She cared about him. She realized that now. She had stayed with him both nights, dozing restlessly on the couch beside him. Every time the door opened, she drowned the doctors and nurses in questions about his prognosis until the staff had learned to enter only when she was sleeping.

The door opened silently. Andie straightened when a nurse—was her name Anne?—slipped quietly inside. As the woman turned, she stifled a gasp of surprise when she saw

Andie jump to her feet and glanced down at the woman's name pinned to her chest. Anne Sampson. She had been right. Before Andie could open her mouth to ask about Tanner's health, the nurse quickly replied, "There's been no change in his health, Mrs. Thornburg."

"Isn't there something more that can be done?"

The nurse hurried around the bed, towels piled high in her arms. She set them down on the table beside Tanner. "The Governor needs a bath. Perhaps you can go home and rest. You haven't slept well in two days."

"I'm not leaving him, Ms. Sampson."

The nurse sighed as she set a razor down beside the towels. She carried an empty pan into Tanner's private bathroom and returned with hot water.

"I'll do the bath." Andie held out her hand. "I'm Tanner's wife. I'll do it."

"Sure, Mrs. Thornburg." Anne placed the washcloth in Andie's hands before leaving the room.

Pulling a chair up to his bed, Andie sat down. She lowered the white sheet covering Tanner's body and then untied the hospital gown. She slid it down his body, slowly exposing his neck, shoulders, chest and belly.

Her breath trembled more than her hands as her gaze consumed every inch she exposed. She trailed her finger across Tanner's jaw, feeling the rough stubble against her palm. Lowering her hand down the column of his throat, she hesitated at his Adam's apple and circled it slowly with her thumb.

Andie's hands stopped where the sheet was gathered at his waist. She silently cursed herself as she drew her hands away. She was acting like a hormonal teenager. And she was taking advantage of an unconscious man. An unconscious, *injured* man who had nearly died saving her.

She returned to the task at hand.

As she grabbed the razor and shaving cream, she cleared her throat nervously as if she had been caught ogling his body. Squirting shaving cream into her hands, she lathered it and applied it to his face.

She lifted the razor. She had never shaved a man before. Was it like shaving her legs? Where should she begin?

Andie carefully applied the razor to his jaw, her eyes narrowed as she tried to concentrate on her job instead of the sharp angles and planes of his face. She gently pulled his upper lip down as she shaved beneath his nose. Turning his face left and right, she shaved his cheeks and jaw.

When she was done, she sat back and rubbed away the remaining cream, revealing a clean, fresh face so handsome it took her breath away.

Reaching for the pan of water, Andie wrung out the washcloth. The water was starting to cool and as she applied the cloth to his chest, goose bumps formed on his chest and shoulders.

She washed his arms, arms that had held her securely, seductively at times, and then turned to his face that she couldn't seem to take her eyes off. And when she was done washing his upper torso, she lifted her hand and squeezed the gown that was bunched in his lap, gathering the courage to remove it completely.

She held her breath and ripped it off Tanner's lap, revealing his body.

Her gaze trailed down his body quickly, as if the task was taking too long. Then she looked again, this time slowly, leisurely slow, studying the hard ridges of his flat belly, the way his waist tapered to the junction of his thighs.

Guilt replaced desire when she saw the bandages on his abdomen. She closed her eyes as she remembered the sound of the gunshot, his blood on her hands.

Her gaze wandered down his belly and her curiosity forced her to look at the part of him that made him male. She reached out and then hesitated with her hand in mid-air. How could she do this to Tanner when he was hurt and unconscious?

Her hand sagged limply into her lap.

"That disappointing, huh?"

Andie gasped loudly. She didn't remember standing.

Didn't remember backing away. But she found herself across the room, her back nestled in the window blinds, her hands covering her blush.

Tanner's eyes were open. He smiled lazily at her.

He had been awake the whole time.

"You—you're…"

"I'm awake," he whispered, his smile broadening. "And in a minute, you would have found out just how alert I was."

"I—I was…I mean, I thought—"

"Andie, it's okay."

"I—I was giving you a bath!"

He laughed so hard it hurt. "Well, I'm not complaining, believe me." He covered himself modestly and looked up at her, waggling his fingers. "Come here."

She shook her head.

"Dammit, Andie, please…just come here."

She edged closer, but not enough to appease him. When he struggled to sit up and grab her, she placed her hands on his shoulders. "Tanner, stop! Don't move, you'll hurt yourself."

"Help…me up." He grimaced in pain. "I want…to see if you're all right and I can't see anything…lying on my back."

She pushed him back on the bed. "Just be still. You're in no shape to move."

Tanner collapsed on the bed and lifted his hand, cupping her jaw. "Are you all right? Did he hurt you?" His fingers stroked her jaw and then lowered to curl around her throat.

Andie brushed his hair from his face. "I'm fine, thanks to you. You saved my life."

"How long have I been here?"

"Almost three days." Andie poured Tanner a glass of water and held it to his mouth, cradling his head as he drank. "I should tell the doctor you're awake."

As she lowered the glass and turned away, he grasped her hand. "Brian…is he…"

"Dead?" She lifted her eyebrows. "Yes."

He fisted his fingers so tightly, his knuckles paled. "Did

he…touch you before I got there?"

Andie shook her head. All tension left his body as he sank into the pillows and whispered, "Thank God."

"I should tell the doctor that you're all right," she repeated and left the room. When she returned, Tanner answered the doctor's questions and tolerated an examination before he and Andie were left alone once again.

Tanner patted the empty spot next to him on the bed. "Sit." She pulled the covers up to his chin. "You should rest." Tanner grasped her elbow. "Don't leave." His hand curled around hers. He brought it slowly to his mouth and lowered his lips to her knuckles.

"Tanner, you shouldn't…" But words failed her as he turned her hand over and kissed the inside of her wrist.

Liquid heat shot through her veins like electricity and settled between her legs. He nipped at the tip of her index finger before inserting it into his mouth. His tongue lavished her finger before turning his attention to her thumb.

Andie pulled her hand away. "Tanner, you have to rest."

She had begun to cherish that boyish grin. "From the looks of those shadows under your eyes, so do you." Before she could react, he pulled her down beside him.

Tanner wrapped his arm around her and closed his eyes, burying his face in her hair. "I thought I would lose you that night." He guided his thumb across the curve of her eyebrow. His eyes filled with desire as he closed the gap between their lips. He kissed her with a passion that startled her. Grinding his mouth against hers, she elicited a moan of pleasure and responded to him just as passionately, her hands cupping his face. She opened her mouth under his and let his tongue plunge inside to mate with hers.

She had misjudged him. He was not weak and helpless as she had thought. His iron strength was evident in the way he kissed and touched her. But when he groaned, she thought it was from pain, not pleasure.

She drew away. "Tanner, we can't do this. You're hurt.

I won't risk—"

The door burst open. They both jumped in surprise as Ron Schultz appeared in the doorway. He stepped through the door and left it to close behind him.

"Ron." Tanner grimaced as he sat up. "What can I do for you?"

Andie straightened and climbed to her feet. She glared at Ron and backed away, as one would when confronted by an unpredictable animal.

Ron met her eyes. "We need to talk."

Andie crossed her arms. "It can wait."

Ron looked only at Tanner as he said, "It's urgent."

"My God, Tanner just regained consciousness!" Andie cried. "Whatever it is, it can wait!"

"I know." Ron stepped forward to squeeze Tanner's shoulder. "I just heard. Thank God you're all right. You gave us all a good scare."

"What do you need?" Tanner asked.

"I need to speak to you, sir."

"Then speak."

Ron nodded toward Andie. "It's regarding her."

"Whatever you have to say, you can say to both of us."

"The incident, the shooting, is in all the papers. Phelps' connection with Andra's past is on the front of all of New York's papers."

Tanner reached for the half-empty glass of water. "Your point?" He brought the glass to his lips and drained it.

"It won't be long until they do a little more digging and discover her past."

"I don't care," Andie said, refilling the glass for Tanner.

"No, you wouldn't, would you?" Ron snapped.

Andie lifted her chin. "What does that mean?"

"Come on, Andra, you don't care about Tanner or his re-election. If you did, you would never put him in this difficult position!"

Tanner leaned forward so fast he gasped and clenched

his side.

Andie rushed forward and pushed him back against the pillow.

"You bastard!" Tanner managed to get out between clenched teeth before Andie turned on Ron.

She hurried across the room and stood in front of him, close enough to see a speck of dry toothpaste caked at the corner of his mouth. "Get out, get out right now!"

"I'm only looking out for your husband, Andra," Ron said. "I'm only thinking of what's best for him and his—"

"What's best for me is her, Ron, can't you understand that?"

Ron met Tanner's narrowed eyes. "You were foolish to do what you did two nights ago. You risked your life and possibly your career!"

Andie clenched her jaw. "He saved my life, you heartless bastard!"

Ron turned and left as quickly as he had come.

~ Twenty-Six ~

Andie opened Tanner's bedroom door and slipped inside to check on him. After arriving home that morning, she hustled him up to the penthouse to rest and recover. Despite his protests, he crawled into bed. He was asleep when she returned with his lunch minutes later.

She'd left the tray of food next to the bed if he should wake but as she walked closer, she saw it still perched on a book he'd been reading in the hospital. His food was untouched, cold by now.

She heard a slight rustle of bedcovers as she stopped beside the bed.

She stilled. "Tanner, are you awake?"

"Andie…" he half-whispered, half-groaned.

"Tanner, are you okay?" She turned on the lamp. Light glowed across the bed.

Tanner was turned away, curled on his side. All she saw

were dark tufts of hair above the blanket.

"Tanner?" She sank into the mattress and as she drew the blankets down, Andie frowned. Tanner's face was flushed scarlet. Sweat beaded his brow. His eyes were clenched tightly. Andie cupped his forehead and softly cursed. He was burning up.

Grabbing the covers, Andie threw them off. Her gaze skipped down Tanner's body. His black T-shirt and boxer shorts were plastered to his body.

Andie pulled up his shirt. Peeling away the bandage that covered his wound, she saw red streaks blazing through it. It could be infected.

She grappled through a tray full of tissues, a bowl of cold soup and a TV remote until she came to the thermometer. Grabbing it, she slipped it between his parched, cracked lips. As she waited, she smoothed back his hair.

"Tanner? Can you hear me?"

He rolled his head toward her but did not open his eyes.

"Tanner, you have to wake up. We have to get you back to the hospital." She ran her hands down his arms, hot and flushed under her touch. Bending over, she ripped off his socks and plucked the thermometer from his lips, bringing it closer to read.

One hundred and three. She must get him cooled down. Now. Quickly.

Rushing into the bathroom, Andie began filling the tub with cold water. As it began to fill, she gingerly stuck her hand into the rising water and bit her lip from the cold. It should work to lower the fever that he battled.

During her tour, she remembered Elizabeth explaining that it was a Jacuzzi and remembered the buttons on the outside of the tub. She pushed one and the water rumbled to life.

The bathroom was the same layout as hers. She crossed to the linen closet separating the Jacuzzi from the shower, console and toilet. Opening a closet door, she pulled out a bath towel and washcloth, placing them on the corner of the Jacuzzi.

Andie returned to the bedroom and sat on the bed. "Tanner? I'm going to need your help getting you into the bathroom."

His eyelids fluttered open. "Andie?"

"Do you think you can stand?"

"I'm...hot."

"I know, sweetheart. You're burning up. I need your help to get you in the bath, okay?"

He closed his eyes, and she feared he would fall asleep again. She leaned over and shook him. "Get up, Tanner." She tugged him to a seated position. Slipping her arm under his, she helped him as he stood on shaky legs. When he rose to his full height, his weight almost toppled them both over, but Andie recovered her footing and helped him into the bathroom.

Tanner swayed weakly and Andie tightened her grip around his waist. She quickly shut off the water and grabbed the bottom of his T-shirt, dragging it off his body. His eyes were open, but he didn't seem aware of where he was or that he was standing half-naked in front of her.

When she peeled off his shorts, she averted her eyes and guided him toward the tub. His foot tangled with the bathmat and he stumbled, almost falling.

He was too weak. He could slip beneath the water. She had to get in the water with him.

She leaned him against the wall. "Lean against this for a minute."

He pressed his cheek against the wall. "I—I'm fine. I just need to—"

"You aren't fine. You're going to the hospital if I can't cool you down." Andie quickly undressed and returned to guide him to the tub. "Do you think you can get in by yourself?"

Tanner stepped unsteadily on the first step, the second, and dropped his foot into the tub. He gasped and immediately withdrew it.

"It's...freezing!"

"It'll help reduce your fever."

"I can't..."

"Get in. I'll follow you to make sure you don't hurt yourself."

He stepped one foot into the tub. The second followed. He gasped again as he lowered himself into the chilly water and huddled with his knees against his chest.

Andie quickly followed him in, echoing his gasp as her foot made contact with the frigid water. As she slipped behind him, she was too cold to care about her nakedness.

She lowered herself in the water, straddling him from behind. Raising her arms, she let him sink into them. She lifted her chin, resting it on top of his head. Lowering one hand, she cupped handfuls of water and cooled his chest, trying to draw the fever from his hot skin.

"Better?"

"No. I'm freezing."

Andie grabbed the washcloth and plunged it under the water. She drew it up and over Tanner's back, watching his muscles twitch and play at the contact. Water ran in rivulets down his bare back before dripping into the water. She repeated the movement over and over again, rinsing his shoulders, his back, his neck, trying to draw the fever out.

"I don't know what else to do, Tan, I'm sorry." Her voice shook and she blamed it on the water but knew it was from emotions. Her throat tightened. She had already lost him once; she couldn't lose him now.

She loved him. She realized that now. The feeling was alien, intense, frightening. Before, all she could think about was leaving. Now, she couldn't imagine being anywhere else but here.

Tanner hissed as she soaped up his wound and washed it gently but thoroughly.

"Jesus, Andie, what are you doing?"

"It's infected." She bent over to look more closely at the wound. "I'm going to have to put disinfectant on it later."

He grew silent and she looked up to see him contain a shiver. He had been in the bathtub long enough. So had she.

Her lips trembled from the cold. He turned his head and seemed to notice it the same time she did. Reaching out, he stilled her lip with his finger.

"Thank you."

She opened her mouth to tell him she loved him but hesitated. Maybe this wasn't a good time. Maybe he didn't feel the same way. *Oh God, what if he didn't feel the same way?*

"Are you going to be okay if I climb out first?" She clutched his shoulder to steady him as she climbed out and quickly dried herself with a thick towel. After wrapping the towel around her, she helped him from the tub. She wrapped him in another towel and helped dry him before handing him a pair of clean boxers to change into.

Leading him into the bedroom, she made him sit in a chair beside the window as she leaned over to strip the bed. When she had remade the bed, she turned down the covers and patted the bed.

"In you go."

He climbed in slowly. Andie pulled the sheet up to his hips, bared his abdomen and then hurried into the bathroom, emerging with antiseptic. She wet a cotton ball and held it above his wound.

"This may hurt a bit."

He clenched his jaw and turned his head away. "Just get it over with."

She applied the cotton ball to his wound and heard him cry out, saw his body tense as fire swept through his wound. She washed it thoroughly, murmuring apologies until she was finished.

Standing, she slipped into her panties and bra and reached for her jeans when he grabbed her hand. "Don't leave. Please, Andie?"

Andie sighed softly and sat on the bed. "Only until you fall asleep, okay?" She leaned back and slipped her legs under the covers. His arm reached out, snaking around her waist to pull her closer.

She extinguished the light to help him sleep, and relaxed

beside him. He pulled her against his body and slipped his leg between hers, burying his face in her hair.

As she lay there, her eyes became heavy and she lost her battle to stay awake.

~ Twenty-Seven ~

She looked like an angel as she slept, one hand tucked under her cheek, her dark hair spilling like ink over the cream-colored satin pillow.

Tanner rose on his elbow. Lowering his hand to her hair, he caressed the silky tendrils tenderly, mindful not to awaken her.

When he awoke to discover Andie sleeping beside him, he couldn't remember how she had gotten there. And when the sunlight played into the room and revealed her near nakedness, he at first couldn't breathe. A variety of emotions ran their course. Shock. Desire. Confusion. Finally anger when he tried to recall last night and couldn't.

Had they made love last night? How could he not remember? He had dreamed of having her in his bed, of making love to her, first with his hands, then with his mouth, finally with his body.

Had he missed out on *everything?*

Andie shifted and stretched her arms over her head. The sheet slipped away, revealing one ripe breast that strained at the fabric of her bra. Tanner curled his fingers under the sheet as desire stirred to life. He tried to resist the temptation to cover her breast with his hand and mold it against his palm.

As if she could sense his lustful thoughts, her eyes popped open.

Tanner forced a cheery smile he wasn't quite feeling. "Good morning."

Andie drew the sheet modestly over her body. "I—I must have fallen asleep last night." She started to get up but realized her near state of nudity. She whipped around and saw by his heavy-lidded expression that he had seen. Ripping the sheet from the bed, she wrapped it around her and stumbled around the bedroom, picking up her clothes. When she was dressed, she sank down on the bed beside him. Leaning over, she pulled away the sheet, revealing his wound.

"Looks better," she said, probing it. "How do you feel?"

"Better."

"I want to clean it again with some antiseptic." She grabbed the bottle of antiseptic from the nightstand and uncapped it.

He watched her soak a cotton ball. "What happened last night?"

She lifted her head sharply. "You don't remember?"

"No."

"I came in last night to check on you and found you burning up with a fever. I had to give you a cold bath."

He narrowed his eyes, searching his empty memory of last night. He couldn't remember her undressing or climbing into the tub with him.

She pressed her palm against his forehead. "You feel cooler. I'll call the doctor and ask him to stop by."

"You don't need to. I feel fine." Actually, he felt great knowing that he hadn't missed out on anything. "In fact, let's go out this weekend."

"No. I want you at home, recovering."

"I feel better."

"You had a temperature last night. I'm not going to let you go out in the cold."

"How about Sunday? That will give me two days to recover."

"I guess."

"We can go out, just you and I. No guards. No reporters. Just us, alone."

"What do you have in mind?"

"It'll be a surprise."

"What if you're not feeling—"

"I'll be feeling fine by then," he said, trailing his fingers down her arm. "Just keep Sunday open."

~ Twenty-Eight ~

Sunday finally arrived and Andie found herself as excited as a teenager on her first date. She flipped down the sun visor and studied herself in the mirror. Lifting her hand, she started to run her fingers through her hair but caught herself and stopped, hoping Tanner hadn't seen her primping.

She looked at him from the corner of her eye to see if he had noticed but he was intent on driving, his thumb keeping beat to the music against the steering wheel. He looked handsome tonight; he'd done a little primping himself. His hair, still slightly damp from his shower and brushed away from his forehead, revealed dark eyes that on occasion Andie had caught watching her.

His cologne, a slight musky scent, filled the car, awakening her senses.

They had been driving in silence now for over fifteen minutes, heading into the city.

"You don't get to drive much, do you?"

"Not as much as I'd like. I'm always shuffled around in the limo." His gloved hands flexed around the steering wheel as he maneuvered the car around several cars parked at the curb. "I miss it."

"I thought so." She pressed her head against the headrest and looked out the window. "I've never seen you drive."

"When was the last time you drove?"

"I don't remember."

"I'll let you drive sometime."

"Where are we going?"

He squeezed her jean-clad knee. "It's a surprise."

"Do you think it was a good idea to leave without telling anybody where we're going?"

"Even if we insisted that we wanted to go alone, Jared

would find a way to follow us. He always does."

"He's a good friend."

"The best."

"I just don't want you to get in trouble."

His touch turned erotic as his thumb circled her kneecap. "Don't worry about me, sweetheart. I'm the boss, remember?"

"And I don't want anything to happen to you while we're out. What if someone recognizes us?"

"Nobody will. Why do you think I had you bring your winter gear?" He cocked his head toward the back seat where their gloves, scarves and hats rested.

Andie leaned forward, turning down the heat. "Do you ever get tired of it?"

"Of what?"

"Being in the spotlight all the time. Being followed around like a celebrity. All the reporters and photographers."

"Sometimes. Does it bother you?"

"Yes. I don't see how it doesn't you bother you more."

"Comes with the territory, I guess."

They continued driving until they arrived in the heart of New York City, where Tanner pulled into a parking garage and parked. Climbing out of the car, Tanner opened the rear door and leaned into the backseat, tossing Andie her hat.

Andie slipped the knit hat on, slid her fingers into her leather gloves and zipped up her winter coat. Tanner shrugged into his winter coat, pulled a hat over his head and locked the car. He grabbed her hand and walked down the sidewalk, toward Central Park.

"Where are we going?"

"You'll see."

Horse-drawn carriages appeared around the corner. A line of horses pawed at the snow-covered ground, their breath steady in the cold air as they bobbed their heads in impatience.

Andie squeezed his hand. "Horse-drawn carriages?"

Tanner stopped in front of a carriage. "Climb in."

Andie laughed and climbed onto the seat as Tanner made arrangements with the driver, who introduced himself as Sam Bernstein. When Tanner was done, he climbed in beside her, pulling a heavy wool blanket over their laps. He leaned against her and wrapped his arm around her shoulders, drawing her closer.

"You folks ready?" Sam asked.

"We're ready!" Andie squeezed Tanner's hand as the driver tapped the reins. The carriage jolted forward and for the next thirty minutes, they were given a ride through Central Park.

The snow was coming down lightly, coating everything in a sugary-white mist.

Tanner squeezed her knee. "I have to admit. I had an ulterior motive, getting you out here."

The giddy girlishness from the evening was replaced by a sober look. "What is it?"

"I want to tell you what happened that night you disappeared ten years ago. You've asked a few times now and I've been avoiding it but you have the right to know."

"What happened that night?"

"We were at our favorite restaurant, Donnelly's. We argued about our marriage. It was the first time I told you how I really felt about it. And you."

"How did you feel?"

"I wanted a divorce."

Andie turned away, gazing at the park in the distance. "It was that bad?"

"We weren't getting along," he said. "When I married, I wanted someone to love me for me, not what I could become. And you…well, you were…you had…"

"I'm not like that anymore, Tanner."

"I know. That's why I had to be honest with you."

"Why are you telling me this?"

"For us to have a future, you had to know. I couldn't keep something like that from someone I love." He lifted his head but refused to face her. "I want us to have a future. I want to wake up beside you every morning."

She turned toward him and touched his face. "Tanner, I want the same thing."

He squeezed her gloved hand. "Andie, marry me."

Andie frowned. "Tanner, we are married."

"Let's renew our vows as a way to start over. Say you'll marry me all over again."

Andie reached up to brush away a snowflake that had landed on his eyelash. "I will."

They sealed the promise with a kiss.

~~~~

Andie fell asleep on the way home. She felt Tanner nudge her as he pulled up beside the curb and stopped in front of the apartment.

"Andie, wake up, sweetie. We're home."

Andie lifted her head from where she had dozed against the window. "What time is it?"

Tanner turned off the car, listening to the engine tick and pop as it cooled. "Almost midnight."

"Thank you for tonight, Tan. I loved it."

"I'm glad." He leaned over to kiss her gently on the mouth. Andie lifted her hand and cupped his face, deepening the kiss. She shivered, leaning against him.

He broke the kiss to murmur, "You're cold. Let's get you inside."

They hurried inside, shutting out the winter wind. Tanner handed his keys to the valet and guided Andie toward the elevators. Stepping inside, he punched the button to the top floor.

As it began to rise, she pressed her back against the wall. "I had a wonderful time."

"Me too."

"Well—"

"You—"

They smiled awkwardly as they spoke at the same time.
"Andie, I…" Tanner stepped closer and cupped her face
in his hands. "I don't want to spend tonight alone."

"Me neither." She closed her eyes as his mouth dipped
down to brush hers.

The elevator jerked to a stop and they hurried inside the
apartment. Andie didn't recall how they ended up in each
other's arms. One minute she was shutting the door, the next she
was in Tanner's arms, being loved by his mouth and hands.

She gasped as his hands explored her body, trailing down
her ribs and over the curve of her hips.

His mouth never stopped its assault on her lips as he swung
her into his arms and carried her into his bedroom, depositing her
on the bed. He sank beside her, lifted his hands to her face and
cupped it, his mouth nibbling at her lips, tasting them, testing
them. Andie opened her mouth under his and he savored the warm
silky harbor of her mouth. The daring of his tongue matched hers,
advancing and retreating, growing bolder each time.

She moaned into his mouth as his fingers swept into her
hair, twisting the ebony strands.

Tanner drew away and closed his eyes, resting his forehead
against hers. "Let me show you how much I love you."

Andie tried to speak but could merely nod. It was the
only encouragement Tanner needed. He bent down and swept
her into his arms, cradling her against his chest as he hurried
into his bedroom.

Tanner turned his head, seeking and finding her lips. Their
mouths never parted as he deposited her gently on the bed.
Andie reached up to switch on the lamp and lay down. They
stared at one another in the dim light, as if they couldn't quite
believe what they saw.

Andie turned on her side, tucking her hand under her
cheek. Tanner's eyes swept over her hair and continued down
her pale throat to the crest of her breasts that rose and fell from
her labored, breathless breathing. His fingers fumbled with the
buttons of his shirt before he finally gave up and swept it up

and over his head.

"If you want to stop this, tell me now, while I still have some control."

Andie lifted a hand, beseeching him. "Don't stop, Tanner."

Tanner dropped his belt and shoes on the floor.

Andie studied his bare chest, her eyes continuing their downward assault as his pants parted and fell from his slender hips.

His body was the epitome of powerful masculinity with thick cords of muscles sculpted from exercise.

He was already aroused. He stood beside the bed, so tall and strong, proud and confident. Andie tried to look modestly away from his rigid flesh but failed.

As he stepped closer to the bed, Andie rolled toward the lamp, lifting her hand to turn it off.

Tanner clasped her hand. "No. Leave it on. Please."

"Why?"

He sank on the bed and dropped a kiss on the back of her neck. "I want to look at you. I want to look in your eyes when I make you mine."

His words startled her in their intensity. Andie drew away and gazed up at him, her eyes large and welcoming as his beautifully tapered fingers skimmed down her throat and brushed the curve of her breast.

"You are so beautiful." Tanner's hand trailed up her leg, over her knee and stopped just below the part of her that ached for his touch.

He lifted his dark eyes. They were filled with desire and love as he whispered, "I want to make you mine, Andie. In every way."

She opened her arms to him and Tanner stretched out beside her. He quickly unbuttoned her shirt. He claimed every exposed inch with his mouth. With his tongue, he discovered every mole and freckle that dusted her body.

The shirt fell away, followed by her jeans, revealing her body.

The dim light in the room washed over her like spun gold. Tanner's breath caught in his throat as he studied her for the first time.

She was beautiful. Perfect. Strong, long legs meant to hold a man and drive him insane. Flared hips that would someday carry his child. Breasts just large enough to cup.

Tanner weighed them in his palms. His thumb circled the rosy aureole before plucking her nipple gently until it awakened with desire. He stroked her breasts until they swelled from his touch. Until her nipples beckoned for his mouth. Until her body cried out for his.

Tanner's hands grew impatient. He lowered his mouth to replace them. With seductive slowness, he sipped lightly at first, sampling first one delicate peak and then the other.

Andie felt an electric current charge through her body. She arched against him, begging him to not stop, wanting something she couldn't identify. Her hands delved into the soft strands of his dark hair.

She cried out his name again and pulled his hair, dragging his mouth back to hers. As he obeyed her silent command to kiss her, Tanner reminded himself to take it slow, but his body rebelled. His erection was painfully tight, throbbing for completion as it strained against her.

He dragged his lips down her body and stopped on her belly. His tongue darted in and out of her navel, circling round and round.

Tanner closed his eyes and fought for control, but he couldn't wait any longer. His body screamed for fulfillment. His hand lowered to the curve of her hip. Hesitating, he met Andie's dark, heavy eyes, full of passion and love, before slipping his hand through the soft nestle of curls that shielded her femininity, to the part of her that was wet and ready for him. Andie gasped as he gently parted and tenderly probed her source of passion.

He watched her face as a rage of emotions crossed it—surprise, delight, shock, fulfillment. He continued stroking her, feeling her tense from a building climax. His breath became ragged as he felt her climax begin even before she became aware of what was happening.

Her eyes flew open in surprise as her body gave in to the whirlwind, explosive release that was building up.

"Tanner…"

He silenced her whisper with his mouth and continued guiding her to completion.

And when it happened, he was more ready than she was. She craned her head back as her body bucked against him, a soft moan escaping her mouth as she ascended steadily toward euphoria.

She collapsed against him, her eyelids too heavy to lift, her body liquid as she returned to earth. Tanner kissed her, rousing her again, until she opened her eyes.

He slowly drew up over her, never breaking contact with her lips, never ceasing his hand as he made her ready for him. He slipped his knee between her thighs and brushed his arousal against her. Without hesitating any longer, he plunged into her and began to move, slowly at first. When they settled into a steady rhythm, he matched her moan for moan, thrust for thrust.

Together, they rode a wild, erotic ride. Tanner rose above her and thrust into her until he could feel his own completion nearing.

She tensed from another building climax. But this time she wasn't alone. He followed her as they both rocketed to the heavens.

~ Twenty-Nine ~

His office phone rang the next morning as Tanner worked at his desk. "Hello?"

"Governor Thornburg, this is Elliott Newman from the *New York Times*—"

"How did you get my office number?" All calls were supposed to be screened before being forwarded to his office.

Elliott ignored his question as he said, "Governor, I was hoping we could meet sometime to discuss your wife, Andra, and her transition—"

"Mr. Newman, I've told you before that my wife is off limits. Can't you people respect that?"

"Where has she been for ten years, Governor? Why the sudden reappearance, right before election year?"

"No comment, sir."

"The people have a right—"

Tanner hung up just as someone knocked on the door.

"Come in." He didn't look up from the tower of paperwork stacked on the corner of his desk. Papers had fallen to the floor from his repeated searches for specific documents. Dozens now rested around his chair.

He had been studying the state budget now for almost four hours, trying to find a way to increase funding for the homeless shelters. Perhaps if they delayed the new laptops that were slated for the teachers for another year...

His office door popped open and Ron stepped inside.

Tanner stopped writing. "What can I do for you, Ron?"

"I need to talk to you."

"Can't it wait? I'm awfully busy with the budget."

Ron's brow furrowed as he closed the door behind him. "Why are you going over the budget? I thought we did that weeks ago."

"I wanted to look at it again."

"I thought it was all set to be approved by the—"

"Not yet." Tanner tapped his pen against the notepad. "I wanted to see if I could delay some spending until next year."

"To do what?"

"Increase funding for the homeless shelters."

"You think that's wise?"

Tanner sighed. "Don't start."

"What? I was just asking, just trying to understand where you're coming from."

"Sometimes I wonder the same about you."

"I think perhaps she's beginning to affect you and your campaign."

"Andie?"

"Who else?"

"I don't care what you think."

"I'm only concerned about you keeping your job in the fall. I don't want to see you make a mistake."

"You call feeding and clothing the homeless a 'mistake'? Giving them a place to stay until they can get on their feet again?"

"Where do you think you'll get this money to increase funding for the homeless shelters?"

"I was thinking of delaying the laptops to the teachers," Tanner replied. "Just until next year."

"You'll lose half your support! The teachers' union helped get you elected—"

"I don't care. The state has cut spending to the homeless now for six years. Numerous shelters have been closed down because lack of funding. It's time we help people who need it."

"This wouldn't happen to be Andra's idea, would it?"

"I think you need to leave."

"Speaking of Andra, what is this nonsense I hear about you doing a fund-raiser for the homeless?"

"Andie has arranged for us to sleep in boxes for two days, outside a homeless shelter to raise awareness and money for the homeless. All proceeds raised would go toward the shelter Martha runs."

"Where did she come up with this hair-brained idea? And what were you thinking, agreeing with it?"

Tanner leaned back and folded his arms. "It was my idea."

Ron's eyebrows lifted as he sank into the chair across from Tanner's desk. "Yours?"

"Mine."

"Why on earth would you want to do that? My God, sleeping in boxes? Have you completely lost your mind?"

"It's two days, Ron, for a good cause."

"When are you doing this?"

"Friday and Saturday night."

"Friday and Saturday! Why didn't you tell me first before you planned it?" Ron said. "You have a campaign dinner Saturday night with—"

"Cancel it," Tanner said. "And I didn't know that I had to seek your approval for anything."

"I am your campaign manager."

Tanner stood up, looming over Ron. "You *were* my campaign manager."

Ron leaned forward in the chair. "What?"

"You heard me," Tanner said. "You're fired."

Ron's mouth sagged in disbelief before he recovered with an arrogant smile. "You can't fire me! On what grounds?"

"For being a cold, selfish bastard."

Anger replaced arrogance. Ron jumped to his feet and slapped his hands on Tanner's desk. "You can't fire me!"

"I just did," Tanner said, sinking back into his chair. "Now go clear out your office. I want you gone by the end of the day."

Ron backed up with hands fisted next to his thighs. "You'll regret this, Thornburg!"

"My only regret is waiting so long to fire you!"

"You're nothing without me, Tanner. You'll soon discover that. You got here today because of me!" Ron said, opening the door. "I'll make you regret this!"

~~~~

"Did you ever...do this?" Tanner said softly, burrowing further into his sleeping bag. He stretched his long frame out and rested his face in his hand as he studied her. "I mean, when you were on the street?"

Andie ducked away from the opening in the box where she was watching the crowd outside gather, and looked at him over her shoulder. "Sleep in boxes?"

Tanner's look was solemn as he met her eyes, as if he

didn't want to know the answer. "Yes. Did you?"

"No," Andie replied, slipping back into her sleeping bag. "I never did although I knew a lot who did." She reached for the zipper and drew it up her body, sealing off the bite of January air. "There was once this guy who was turned away because the shelter couldn't take anymore that night. They found him frozen to death inside a..." She trailed off, not wanting to call up that memory. "He had been there a week before someone found him. He was frozen to the ground; it was awful."

"Where would you stay?"

"Shelters. That's why this is so important. People need to realize that the homeless are not something to fear, that they're human just like everybody else. They only have the misfortune to be down on their luck."

A battery-operated light in the corner of the box flickered, threatening to go out. Andie stared at it without blinking, caught in a trap of terrible memories.

Tanner reached across the cramped space and grabbed her hand as if to pull her back from the precipice of the past. "It's important to me too."

"I'm glad."

"I'm going to try to get more funding for the shelters. Maybe we can open the ones that were previously closed."

Andie lifted her head. "Really?"

"It's going to take some changes in the budget but I think it'll pass."

"You would do that, Tanner?"

"Of course, Andie."

"It would mean so much to me but I hope that's not why you're doing it."

"I'm doing it because it's the right thing."

A moment of silence passed between them before he said, "Tell me about it. About what it was like living on the streets."

So she did. She told him about the survival on the streets. Always walking around with an empty, growling stomach.

Eating one meal a day if lucky. Being kicked by a group of teenagers who teased them unmercifully.

When she was done, he reached out and pulled her into his arms and held her. As he stroked her hair, she listened to the noise, to the world, outside. She heard reporters shouting questions from behind the barricades the police had set up along the curb. The squawk of police radios as they patrolled the area, keeping vigilant watch.

Tanner had given a quick interview to a number of reporters before crawling into the box that had once been used to transport a refrigerator.

A local radio station, their live broadcast being heard from where they camped out on the corner of the street, asked for citizens to come down and help the cause. And people turned out by the carloads. Martha manned a table in front of the shelter where people could donate money. The homeless mingled among the crowd, serving hot chocolate and donuts donated by local businesses.

All in all, it looked to be going very well.

Andie shuddered in the cold. Tanner must have seen her tremble because he threw back the top of his sleeping bag.

"Come on in. I'll warm you up."

Andie crawled out of her sleeping bag and into his. She sat up and arranged her sleeping bag over them both for extra warmth. She snuggled closer, feeling his body heat penetrate her backside.

"Thank you for doing this."

He bent his head and kissed the side of her neck. "I'm glad to."

She craned her head back, looking up at him. "I hope you didn't do it for me, Tanner."

"*We* did it for them." Tanner stressed the word as he looked out the box at a homeless man visiting with a crowd of teenagers in the front of the line. The man handed the three teens cups of hot chocolate; Tanner saw steam rolling off the cups. He turned to Andie. "And I did it because I love you and want to make you happy. I won't deny that."

She nervously fingered the zipper of her sleeping bag. "I—I love you too."

Glancing up, Tanner could hear but not see the news helicopters hovering overhead as they captured the moment on film. They competed with police helicopters, which patrolled the sky as they kept close watch on the crowd below.

Never before had a governor done this. The charity event had been well publicized weeks before, the proof being the huge turnout today and the $40,000 already collected at drop-off centers around town prior to the event.

Tanner had never been more proud of the people of New York than he was at that moment. He grinned. "You know, this is the best part of my job, being able to help people and make positive changes like this."

"Do you like your job, Tanner?"

"Yes, because I can help those who need it."

"I was thinking of volunteering down at Martha's shelter maybe once a week."

"I think that would be great."

Jared appeared with a box of donuts in his hands. He leaned down, offering one to each of them. "I come, offering food."

Andie plucked a glazed donut from the box. "Thanks, Jared." She licked the glaze off her fingers.

"Thanks," Tanner said, picking a sprinkled donut from the box.

Jared closed the box. "There's an Elliott Newman from the *New York Times* here, saying you granted him an interview. Is that right?"

Tanner rarely granted interviews to the press. He usually informed the public of news and information through press releases or conferences. A personal interview was highly sought after by the media and often turned down.

Except today. Today was important.

"Elliot Newman?" Andie said. "The guy who scared me half to death in the parking garage?"

"The one and only," Tanner mumbled. "Why did it have to be Newman?"

"I'm sorry, Tanner, "Andie said. "When I asked for someone at the paper to cover this, I didn't know—"

"It's not your fault," he replied. "Newman would give away his first born to have this story."

Andie caught Jared scowling.

She glanced warily at the guard. "I thought it would be a good way to bring more awareness to the situation."

"It's fine," Jared replied. "I'll escort him through and be back in a minute."

They moved outside the box to conduct the interview. Andie frowned as Jared escorted Elliott Newman through the crowd. The reporter was wearing black again. Was it the only color the man owned?

He was followed by a tall, lanky man, clutching a camera. Both men stopped in front of them.

Andie stood. "Elliott," she said, greeting him coolly.

Elliott shifted his pen and notebook into his other hand to offer his hand. "Nice to see you again, Mrs. Thornburg. It's a real pleasure." His eyes could be called green, Andie guess, but were so pale that it was hard to tell.

Tanner reached out his hand. "Evening, Elliott."

"Governor, sir, how are you?" Elliott looked over his shoulder at the man standing behind him. "Pete Johnson, my photographer. He's going to be in the background, snapping some shots. Don't mind him."

Tanner smiled and swept his hand toward the ground. "Take a seat, Mr. Newman."

Elliott sank on the ground, across from Andie and Tanner, and folded his legs Indian-style. "Thank you for allowing me to see you. I've been trying for three years."

Tanner smiled tightly. "I know."

Elliott opened a tattered spiral notebook and paused with his pen on the paper. As he started to write, Andie leaned closer and saw him scribble the date and time. The photographer stepped away and drifted around them, snapping pictures.

"I have to remind you that you're here only to report the charity event," Tanner said. "I won't discuss anything else."

Elliott paused with the pen on the paper. "Of course, Governor." He cleared his throat and glanced between Tanner and Andie. "Maybe you can start by telling me how this came about?"

"The city has an epidemic on its hands, Elliott," Tanner replied. "More and more homeless shelters are closing, leaving people with nowhere to go. We thought we could raise awareness as well as some money to help them in any way we can."

"How much have you raised so far?"

"According to the last count, over forty thousand," Andie said. "We have dozens of drop-off centers where people can stop to make a donation if they can't make it downtown."

Elliott lifted his eyebrows. "That's a lot for only your first day."

"The radio stations and local television channels have been so cooperative and generous with this," Andie replied. "We wish to thank them for all their help and time in promoting this event."

Tanner nodded. "And we'd especially like to thank the people of New York. They've been so generous with not only their money but their time."

"They've offered to volunteer at the shelters and if some can't afford to drop off money, they donate other items like furniture," Andie said.

A sly smile curled Elliott's lips as he met Tanner's eyes. "It's ironic that you cut funding for the shelters two years ago and now you're here today."

Andie glanced at Tanner, her brow lifted.

Tanner cleared his throat. "It's unfortunate, I know, but sometimes things in the budget have to be reduced in order to afford education and other social services such as Medicare and Medicaid."

"But you didn't reduce funding, Governor, you cut it completely, causing two shelters to close their doors," Elliott said. "A lot of people say you're doing this only to get votes for the fall election. That you didn't care about the homeless three years ago when you cut funding, and you don't care now. The only things you care about are votes."

"This has absolutely nothing to do with my re-election. It's because I care—"

"So much so that you left them on the streets?"

"Elliott, if this is going to turn into this, I'm ending the interview now."

Elliott leaned forward. "Can you tell me why your campaign manager, Ron Schultz, was let go a few weeks ago?"

"I have no comment on that."

Elliott looked at Andie. "Can you tell me, Mrs. Thornburg, where you were these past ten years?"

Andie opened her mouth to reply but Tanner snapped, "Leave her out of it. She has nothing to say, and neither do I. This interview is over!"

"Some people are saying that Andra's sudden reappearance was staged to bring in more votes and assure you another win. What is your comment on that?"

"I'd call it absurd."

Andie frowned. "I thought we were here to talk about the charity event."

Elliott leaned forward, a predatory look in his eyes as he looked at Andie. "Can you tell me why you really disappeared ten years ago, Mrs. Thornburg?" He lifted his eyebrows. "There was no kidnapping, was there? Wasn't it staged to assure Tanner a win in the elections?"

Tanner jumped to his feet. "That's enough! I won't listen to any more of your accusations!"

He glanced up and waved Jared over, who hovered close by to keep an eye on his boss.

Jared hurried over. "Is he bothering you, sir?"

"Take him and his photographer away, Jared."

Jared clamped a hand around Elliott's elbow, dragging him to his feet. "Come with me, sir."

Elliott glanced at Tanner over his shoulder as Jared pushed him away. "I will find out the truth, Governor."

"You're wasting your time," Tanner said. "There's nothing to find out!"

As Jared pushed Elliott through the crowd, the reporter straightened and ripped his elbow away. "Okay, okay. Mind giving me my arm back?"

Jared crossed his arms as he watched Elliott stumble away. "Don't bother disturbing the Governor again, got it?"

"Yeah, yeah," Elliott mumbled, walking down the sidewalk.

As he paused on the corner to cross the street, he thought he heard his name being called. He looked around, eyes traveling down the line of people curling around the corner, waiting to make a donation. He saw nobody he recognized.

A motion. On the other side of the street.

Elliott peered closer.

A man waving his arms, trying to get his attention.

The light turned green and people started crossing the street. As Elliott drew closer, he recognized him.

Ron Schultz.

~ Thirty ~

The phone next to the bed jangled shrilly, jarring Tanner from sleep. He opened his eyes on the first ring, rolled over on the second, and was reaching for the phone during the third, trying to grab it before Andie woke up.

He fumbled for the receiver with clumsy fingers and as he brought it to his ear, looked over at his wife. Only the top of her head could be seen above the covers but she didn't stir. She was still asleep, trying to catch up on what she had lost over the weekend. It had been a long, exhausting three days for both of them but well worth the nearly $200,000 they had raised.

"Y—Yes?" he whispered, clearing his sleep-laced voice.

"Governor?" Elizabeth Van Dyke said softly. "I'm in the lobby. I think we need to talk."

"Now?" Tanner glanced at the clock that glowed red on the bed stand. Ten o'clock on a Sunday morning? He hadn't slept this late since college.

He cleared his throat again. "Can't it wait?"

"I'm afraid not, sir."

"Is something wrong?"

"Can I come up? We can talk about it then."

"Sure. I'll see you in a minute." Tanner hung up and crawled out of bed. He reached down, grabbing the jeans beside the bed. After getting home around midnight, they were too exhausted to do much more than collapse in bed.

He stepped into his jeans and slid them up and over his boxers before zipping them. He leaned over his wife, kissing her hair softly and brushing it away from her face before entering the bathroom.

He quickly splashed water on his face to help him wake up and brushed his teeth before entering the living room. A minute later, Elizabeth knocked lightly on the door and he let her in. A newspaper was folded in her hands.

"Let's go into the kitchen so I can start some coffee to help me wake up," he said, motioning her to follow him.

Tanner yawned as he crossed to the refrigerator. Opening it, he grabbed the orange juice and drank from the bottle, emptying what little remained before reaching in for a new bottle and twisting the cap.

"What do you need on a Sunday morning, Elizabeth, that can't wait until tomorrow?"

Elizabeth folded the newspaper. "Have you seen the paper yet this morning?"

"Of course not. I just woke up after three days of being cooped up in a box the size of my refrigerator." Tanner poured some orange juice into a glass. "Why?"

"I think you need to read this." She pushed the newspaper

across the granite countertop.

Reading the headline, Tanner stopped with the glass halfway to his lips.

Mystery Solved! Investigation Reveals Homelessness, Criminal Activity in Wife's Past. Under that, the subtitle: *Governor's Wife Lived Homeless for Ten Years.*

Ron. This was his doing.

"Sir, do you want to read it?"

"No."

Elizabeth pointed to the byline at the top of the article. "Elliott Newman revealed everything. Where Andie was living, what she was doing, where she stayed, her criminal record, her medical records. Everything."

Tanner flexed his fingers around the glass. He was tempted to hurl it against the ceramic tile floor.

"Sir?"

"It was Ron."

"Sir, this could affect—"

"I don't care!"

"You need to consider having a press conference. Try to explain that you wanted this to be a private ordeal and hope that voters will understand."

"I don't care what they think."

Elizabeth picked up the remote and switched on the television that sat on the countertop at the other end of the room.

"—not quite sure how this will affect his approval ratings and it's really too soon to tell," a field reporter was saying into the camera. "Back to you, Carolyn."

"Thank you, Keith." The camera switched back to a woman seated in the television studio. "This is Carolyn O'Connor, from Channel 6 News. Coming up...Dan Brown with the weather."

"Turn it off," Tanner muttered.

Elizabeth flipped to another local news channel.

"—and if he withheld this, what else is he hiding from us?" said a man on the street as a microphone was thrust in his face.

Tanner plucked the remote from her hands and turned off the television.

"We should have just come out with it the minute we found her," Elizabeth said. "It'll look like you tried to cover it up."

"I was trying to protect her."

"Protect me from what?" Tanner looked up to see Andie watching them from the hallway. Her face was the color of the white robe she wore. She regarded him with narrowed, suspicious eyes, an expression he hadn't seen since the day he'd found her in jail. Dark circles shadowed her eyes.

Tanner lifted the bottle of orange juice. "Come sit down and have some breakfast," he said, trying to stall before telling her the truth.

She remained where she was, her cheek pressed against the cool doorframe. "What happened?"

Tanner forced a smile that felt stiff and awkward. "Nothing we can't handle, sweetheart. Now come sit down and have something to eat."

Andie stepped into the kitchen. Only the tips of her toes could be seen under the long robe that dragged on the tiled floor as she walked closer. Her arms lifted to cross over her chest. She leaned a hip against the countertop of the island in the center of the room, using it as a barrier.

"What's going on?"

And then she saw the newspaper. When she read the headline, her lips began trembling. "Oh God."

"It'll be okay." Tanner reached across the island but she backed away. "I'm not worried about it and you shouldn't be either."

"It's not me I'm worried about." She reached for the newspaper but Tanner beat her to it and threw it in the garbage under the sink.

"I want to read it!"

"Don't bother." He looked at Elizabeth. "Liz, can you give us a minute? We can talk about this first thing tomorrow."

After Elizabeth left the room, Andie said, "What do they know?"

"Everything, I'm afraid."

"My criminal record?"

"Yes."

Andie sank onto the stool Elizabeth had just vacated. "Oh no." She closed her eyes. "Oh no!"

Tanner stepped behind her and squeezed her shoulders. "Listen, Andie, I don't care that they know or think. And you shouldn't care either."

Andie climbed to her feet and crossed to the sliding glass door, looking out into the backyard. "I don't give a shit what they think about me, Tanner. I never did."

"Then what—"

"I care what they think of *you!*" Andie leaned her forehead against the cool glass pane of the sliding door. "Oh God, what's going to happen now? What will the voters think?"

"Don't say that. You sound like Ron."

Andie buried her fist in her mouth. "This is my fault. If you don't get re-elected—"

"It's *not* your fault. You didn't expose this, Ron did!"

Andie closed her eyes. "What have I done to you? I never meant this to happen. I was only trying to survive back then."

"I know that, Andie, and the voters will too."

~~~~~

The next morning, Tanner looked up from the kitchen table where the morning newspaper sat untouched. "Well, tell me. What's being said?"

Elizabeth nodded toward the newspaper. "You haven't read it?"

Tanner lifted a knife and began cutting his pancakes into tiny squares. "I can't."

"You haven't even watched the news?"

"I don't want to alarm Andie."

"What is she saying about all this?"

"She hasn't left her room since all hell broke loose yesterday."

Despite his pleas to join him, Tanner had slept alone last night for the first time in many nights. The bed felt too big without her; he tossed and turned all night.

Andie had locked herself away in her room since the incident yesterday. The door was still locked when Tanner tried it again this morning, after waking up early to prepare for this morning's meeting.

"That bad?" asked Elizabeth.

"She's blaming herself for all this. Says she's ruined my chances at re-election." Stabbing his pancakes, Tanner brought a piece to his mouth and looked up at his assistant who'd been promoted to fill Ron's spot. "What do you think, Liz?"

She pulled out the chair across from him and sat down. "Honestly? I think you have cause to worry. Your ratings have slipped nearly twelve points."

Tanner lowered his fork. He'd never fallen more than three or four points in his approval ratings. Twelve points was unimaginable.

"The public thinks your wife was a thief and prostitute."

"I'll just tell them—"

"People are distrustful of the government and politicians as it is. Very few will believe you."

"What can be done?"

"You can try calling a press conference to explain but you might just be wasting your time. Voters are very fickle and hard to sway once they've made up their minds." Elizabeth leaned forward in her chair and buried her face in her hands as she added, "This incident—Andie—could have very well just ended any possibility of another term in office."

~~~~~

Andie stepped away from the kitchen door when she heard Elizabeth's words. She closed her eyes and sank against the wall for support. Leaning her head back, she gazed at the cathedral ceilings, blinking away tears.

How could she have done this to Tanner? How would he recover? He would never forgive her. *She would never forgive herself.*

Bowing her head to her chest, Andie gave into silent sobs that shook her body. Bringing a hand to her mouth, she silenced the cries, afraid Tanner or Elizabeth would hear.

She should never have come here. She should have left as soon as she could. Before she had fallen in love with Tanner. Before she had ruined his future.

"You know, this is the best part of my job, being able to help people and make positive changes like this." His words from the night of the charity event came back to haunt her.

Andie closed her eyes. What to do, *what to do?*

They could do as Elizabeth suggested and call a press conference to try to explain the truth but nobody would believe it. Must people might understand the amnesia, the homelessness, the *hopelessness.* But the criminal charges?

No. No way. Nobody would trust a man in office whose wife had a criminal record.

Andie hurried into her bedroom. There was only one thing left to do to save Tanner's career.

~~~~

Elizabeth lifted her face from her hands and looked across the table at Tanner. "What do you want to do?"

Tanner stared over her shoulder.

"Governor?"

Tanner finally blinked.

"Sir?" Elizabeth looked over her shoulder, expecting to see Andie in the doorway again but nobody was there. "I asked—"

"I heard you."

"What are you thinking?"

He blinked again and met her confused eyes. "I'm not going to seek re-election."

"What!" Elizabeth came out of her chair. "Sir, you can't be serious!"

"I am." Tanner pushed his plate away, his appetite lost. "And it feels like a giant weight just lifted off my shoulders."

"But you—you can't give up, you've worked too hard!"

"And for what? My wife to be publicly ridiculed, harassed and teased by so-called 'friends' because she's not like them? Andie has put up with so much from everybody, and why? Why does she do that?"

"I—I don't know. To help you get re-elected?"

"Exactly!" Tanner jumped to his feet and grabbed his plate, carrying it to the dishwasher.

Elizabeth's gaze followed him across the room. "I don't understand."

"She puts up with it because of the election. To make *me* happy. She'll put up with people like Ron, who mock her and judge her, all because of the election. It's wrong, Elizabeth, it's just wrong. She's sacrificed so much for me."

"But, sir, your career!"

Tanner finished loading the dishes in the dishwasher. He looked out the kitchen window above the sink and shoved his hands in his pockets. "I don't want this, Liz. Not anymore. Not if it means putting Andie through that."

"We won't put her—"

"Not even if, by some chance, everything goes back to the way it was. I don't want it anymore. Family is more important than being governor."

~ Thirty-One ~

Her bedroom door hung open.

Tanner glanced down the hallway. Perhaps he should

give her some time alone. *No.* He wouldn't let her feel sorry for herself about this. It was not her fault. He had to get that through to her. They would clear this up, go public with what really happened.

They would face this together.

He wanted to tell her what he'd decided downstairs, how much better he felt when he thought of the normal life they could live for once. Out of the spotlight. Out of the newspapers. She'll feel better too; able to be herself.

"Andie?" Tanner walked in her bedroom. Her closet door lay ajar.

No clothes in the closet.

"You in here?"

No personal items in the bathroom. A towel lay limply by the toilet, the only thing in the bathroom.

"Andie?"

Where had she gone? She hadn't...

He sank on the unmade bed. He could still smell her perfume in the room, on the sheets.

She hadn't left him, had she?

Yes, he realized, she had *for him.* To save *his* reputation, his future, his career. She was unselfish enough to do it.

Tanner hurried from the bedroom and saw Elizabeth getting ready to let herself out.

"Liz, have you seen Andie?"

Elizabeth hesitated with her hand on the doorknob. "No. I thought she was in her room."

"She's not," Tanner said, brushing by Elizabeth and out the front door. "Where's Jared?"

"I haven't seen him yet this morning."

At that moment, Jared stepped off the elevator, a cappuccino clenched in his hand. At Tanner's expression, his bodyguard lowered his cup. "What's wrong?"

"Where have you been?"

"Starbucks."

"Did you go somewhere before that?"

"Tanner, what's wrong? Did something happen?"

"I can't find Andie. Have you seen her?"

"Andie? Yes, I just got back from dropping her off."

~~~~

After climbing off the subway, Andie wandered the streets of New York City for an hour. She considered having Jared drive her to the airport but didn't want Tanner to find out where she had gone. Two hundred dollars was folded in her pocket. Enough for a one-way ticket.

It was getting dark and she was hungry. She pressed a hand against her belly and scanned the street before crossing. Two hundred dollars was a lot of money to be carrying around in this neighborhood. She needed to get off the street and find a place to eat before she headed toward the airport.

She was so hungry, she felt almost sick to her stomach. How long had it been since she had eaten? She couldn't remember. It was like the old days on the street. Except she had money this time. Money and enough clothes to get her by.

A single suitcase trailed behind her, filled with only the necessities to get her by in the next few weeks until she decided what to do next, where to go.

She couldn't go back on the streets. And, she thought as people watched her walk across the street, she would be recognized soon if she stayed around here.

She wore her hair tucked through the back of a baseball cap, the bill and sunglasses shielding her face. After the sun went down, the sunglasses would have to come off. It wouldn't take long before reporters recognized her.

As she stepped off the curb, she looked up to see the homeless shelter ahead. Maybe Martha was in. Maybe she'd have some food.

She would stay a few minutes and then be on her way.

~~~~

"Where did she go, Jared?"

Tanner climbed into the backseat of the limo and his friend took the other side.

"She asked me to drop her off at the subway," he replied. "Said she was going shopping."

The engine purred to life and the limo pulled out of the drive and onto the road.

"Why didn't you stay with her?"

"She wouldn't let me so I trailed her for about ten minutes before she lost me. She must have seen me and ditched me."

Andie was in her element on the streets. If her intent was to get away, she would do just that and employ every skill she had learned from her past to survive.

He wasn't surprised she had managed to slip away from his guard who was every bit as good at following someone without being detected as Andie was at escaping them.

"The subway," Tanner said. "My God, she could go anywhere. Did she say where she was going?"

"No, I wish I could tell you more, sir." Jared leaned over and switched on the miniature television that was positioned across from them in the backseat. He flipped through the channels until he came to the news.

"What are you doing?" Tanner asked.

"With all this hype going on, she'll be recognized sooner or later and it'll be on the news."

Tanner closed his eyes. "I wish you were right but Andie is at home on the streets. If she doesn't want to be found, she won't be."

~~~~~

"Hello, Martha."

Martha Dexter lifted her head and smiled broadly. "Oh Andie, sweetie, how are you?"

Andie managed a smile and walked across the kitchen. "I'm all right."

Martha swept her hand across the room, motioning toward dozens of boxes stacked in the kitchen. "Look at all of this. This is all your doing. You and that hunky husband of yours. You both are dear-hearts for what you did for these people."

Andie walked through the maze of boxes. "What is all this?"

"Boxes of items donated by area businesses." Martha kneeled next to a box and opened it. "Every time we unpack them, more come in. We're running out of room."

Andie peered over the top of an open box. "What do you have here?"

"What you should ask is what we don't have!" Martha replied. "Everything from towels to dinner plates to clothing to food."

"That's great to hear."

Martha stood up and enveloped Andie in a hug. "We can't thank you enough." She stepped back. "Are you here to volunteer? You could start maybe by unpacking some of the boxes and sorting them. We're putting…" Martha stopped when she saw Andie's expression. "What is it, dear?"

"I'm afraid I won't be able to volunteer now."

"Well, that's okay, Andie. I understand. I remember you saying something about coming in over the weekend and just assumed that's why you were here."

"Something's come up, I'm afraid. I'm going to have to leave."

"What? Why? What about the Governor's…" Martha stopped suddenly and planted her hands on her hips. "Wait a minute, here. You guys aren't upset about this coverage, are you? It's absolutely absurd what they're saying about you, Andie. It's nonsense, is what it is."

Andie gazed at her shoes for a moment before looking up. Tears pooled in her eyes. "I'm afraid I've ruined Tanner's chance at re-election."

"That's absurd. The folks who use this shelter deal with

the same things you did back then. I'll come forward and tell the press that this is a problem the homeless deal with as a daily occurrence. People will understand that it's nothing but a lie to make you and the Governor look bad."

"I appreciate it, Martha, I do, but—"

"But nothing, Andie," Martha said, guiding Andie into a chair. "Now sit down before you fall down, and let me make you some dinner. You look like you haven't eaten anything in a week."

~~~~~

Tanner's cell phone vibrated against his hip. He reached for it and brought it to his ear.

"Andie?"

"No, sir, this is Elizabeth."

Tanner leaned against the leather seats of the limo as it sped downtown. "Elizabeth, did Andie return home?"

"I'm afraid not, sir, but I'm calling because—"

"Have you heard anything from her? Has she tried calling home?"

"Well, in fact, I have a Martha Dexter holding on the other line as we speak. You know her?"

"Of course. What—"

"Good, because I thought she was just another reporter trying to—"

"Liz, what does she want?"

"She says that Andie is at the shelter downtown. Ms. Dexter is trying to stall her but is having a hard time convincing Andie to stay. She says to hurry."

~ Thirty-Two ~

Tanner was out the door before the car came to a complete stop. "Wait here for me," he instructed Jared as he hurried inside the shelter.

Martha met him at the door. "Governor, you made it. I'm so glad—"

"Where is she?"

Martha hugged a coat against her chest. Tanner recognized it as Andie's. "She left about fifteen minutes ago. I tried to stall until you could get here but she caught me on the phone, talking to your assistant and left before I could stop her." Martha pushed the coat at her. "Andie left so fast she forgot her coat. The poor girl is out there in the cold without a coat."

"Which way did she go? Did you see?"

Martha pointed east. "I saw her run that way." Martha nodded toward a suitcase inside the front door. "She left behind her suitcase too. If you don't find her, she'll have nothing, Governor, and you know she won't return here for help. Not after what I did. I betrayed her."

Tanner squeezed the older woman's shoulders. "I'll find her." He returned to the limo, climbed inside and motioned for the driver to head east.

He and Jared scanned the sidewalks as they slowly traveled down the road. The neighborhood turned from bad to worse the further they drove. Vagrants cluttered the doorways of area businesses, many of which were abandoned. Litter blew across the street and clogged storm drains. It started snowing again, falling faster and harder, making it difficult to see out the snow-crusted windows.

"We have to find her," Tanner said.

"We will," replied Jared.

"Where would she have gone?"

Jared looked up to see a sign pointing toward the subway. "There."

The limo pulled to the side of the road and both Tanner and Jared climbed out.

Tanner hurried toward the subway. "You can wait in the car. I'll be fine."

Jared eyed the doorways they passed. "I'm not leaving you, not in this neighborhood."

Tanner's coat flapped open in the wind but he was oblivious to the cold. "Oh God, what if something happens to her in this neighborhood? What if someone jumps her? What if—"

"Give her some credit, Tanner. She lived on the streets for ten years. She knows what she's doing."

"You're right," Tanner said as he descended a set of steps.

In the belly of the subway, he scanned the crowd. It was crowded down here for this time of day. It was Monday, not rush hour, but it was already shoulder to shoulder with people.

Some people were waiting in line to get on the subway. Others were down here just to get out of the cold. Tanner and Jared walked through the crowds of people, their heads swiveling as they looked for her.

They had no idea what she was even wearing. And Andie wouldn't have left the house without bringing something to disguise herself in public. He looked for someone wearing a scarf or hat worn low.

He heard the commotion by the tracks and knew he had found her. A crowd of reporters had gathered, forming a wall around someone. Their hurtled questions could be heard and flashing cameras strobed above the crowd.

"It's her," Tanner said, switching from a walk to a run. "It's gotta be."

Jared hurried ahead of him, pushing through the crowd.

As Tanner came closer, the questions came faster and clearer.

"Mrs. Thornburg, do you have a minute—"

"Andra, can you explain the prostitution on your record?"

"Mrs. Thornburg, what does the governor say about your criminal record?"

Tanner pushed a reporter in his rush to get to his wife.

The reporter turned and glared at Tanner. "Hey, watch

it, buddy! Can't you see…" The man's eyes widened. "Hey, it's the Governor."

"Get back, all of you!" Jared shouted, pushing back the crowd as Tanner made his way to his wife.

Tanner could see her pinned against the edge of the tracks with nowhere to escape as the crowd hurtled accusations and questions at her.

She didn't see him coming toward her but looked down at the tracks four or five feet below, as if contemplating jumping down there to escape.

"Mrs. Thornburg, how does your husband think it will affect his chances at re-election?"

One more step and he was beside her. He startled her as he wrapped his arms around her. She jumped at his touch but then murmured his name before burying her face into his chest.

Tanner looked over her head at the reporter who had asked the question.

"You want to know how it'll affect my chances at re-election, sir?"

"Governor!" Reporters rushed forward but Jared pushed them away.

The crowd stirred at Tanner's sudden appearance. Tanner encircled Andie's shoulders and hugged her in a tight bear-hug. She shivered. From the cold or fear? Maybe a little of both, Tanner thought.

He stroked her hair and glared at the reporters. They were a bunch of vultures; he hated every one of them for doing this. To him, they were merciless individuals who only wanted a headline tomorrow.

"You want to know what I think about her criminal record?" Tanner repeated the question. "Is that what you want to know?"

"How do you feel about your wife being a prostitute, Governor Thornburg?"

"I think it's absurd," Tanner replied, "and a ridiculous, trumped-up charge that was put on her record."

"But it was on her record, Governor. You can't dispute that!"

"No, but you can dispute how it got there!" Martha Dexter's voice could be heard above the crowd before she finally appeared in front. "If you look up the records of nearly every homeless person, you will find at least one trumped-up charge!" The woman turned and addressed the reporters. "These individuals are picked up, tormented and harassed by the police on a daily basis, gentlemen, and it's shameful. Andie's generosity and devotion to the homeless are not the actions of a prostitute and thief!"

"How do you think it will affect your campaign, sir?" another reporter asked.

Tanner narrowed his eyes. "The truth is, gentlemen and ladies, I'm not going to run again."

Andie stiffened in his arms and whispered, "Tanner, no!"

He had never before seen reporters speechless and he took a small amount of pride in it. He waited for the shock to pass and the questions to begin once again. And it only took a matter of seconds.

"Sir, can you tell us what brought this about?"

"I've decided that lies, accusations and dirty politics are not worth the misery my wife and I have endured these past few months. I love her too much to put her through another four years of it." He brushed his lips against her hair and whispered, "And you can't make me change my mind, Andie. I'm not happy doing this. Not anymore. Not after what I've seen people do in the name of politics."

She lifted her head and he saw tears streaking down her cheeks.

"My future isn't complete without you in it." He brushed away her tears. "I've made up my mind. I love you too much to put you through this for another four years."

Andie buried her face in his chest. "Oh Tanner, thank you, thank you," she whispered against his coat.

As more questions were directed at them, Andie lifted

her head, glaring at the reporters.

"You all need to focus more on what really matters in society," she said. "Start reporting the real news. Things like what the homeless face every day, not people's private lives!" Standing tall, she slipped her hand inside Tanner's.

Tanner squeezed her hand. "Let's get out of here and go home, what do you say?"

Andie smiled and squeezed back. "I say that's the best thing I've heard in awhile."

Kate Rizor is a former newspaper reporter, editor, copywriter and trainer. She resides in Vicksburg, Michigan with her husband, Steve. She is currently at work on her second novel and conducts fiction and non-fiction seminars and workshops in her spare time.

Kate would love to hear from you at:

katerizor@hotmail.com or
visit www.katerizor.com